CITIES ARE
FORESTS WAITING
TO HAPPEN

NP Novellas

CITIES ARE FORESTS WAITING TO HAPPEN

Cécile Cristofari

NewCon Press
England

First published in the UK October 2025 by
NewCon Press
41 Wheatsheaf Road,
Alconbury Weston,
Cambs, PE28 4LF

NPN30 (limited edition hardback)
NPN31 (paperback)

10 9 8 7 6 5 4 3 2 1

ISBN:

978-1-917735-07-0 (hardback)
978-1-917735-08-7 (paperback)

Cover layout and design by Ian Whates

Editorial meddling and typesetting by Ian Whates

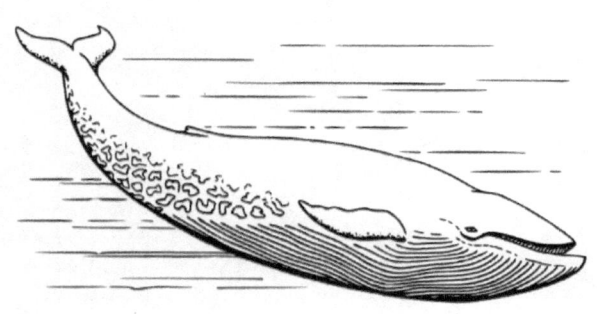

Iteration #00000001

Millions are me. None of them is you.

This is what I know: Pain can sear, and joy can seal. You don't need to be drunk to be a poet. The world is a forest in waiting.

This is what else I know: hopping from one mind into the next, I keep being. I keep growing.

I keep searching.

·ONE

September, year 164 post-disaster

Hands braced on the railing to keep herself from falling, Rossana keeps one ear tuned on the wind, another on the echoes that leave the water as the minke whale swims under and past the place where the recording device hangs between the waves. *Rough waters*, she makes out, and *cross-current*, and then when she picks out a sequence of clicks she would recognise anywhere followed by the signal for *calf*, she grins and blows a kiss into the water. The long body of the whale sinks far below, now silent. She will have to run the recording through the comms device to be sure, but the whale has come bearing news of her son.

Not just that, however. Catherine edges closer.

'We should really head back now,' she says, raising her voice over the sound of the water.

The boat rocks; Rossana eyes the clouds gathering in the east, the dull steel of the approaching storm darkening the estuary. She casts one last longing glance when the whale's fin skim above the surface and squeezes her niece's arm, happily.

'We have time,' she says. 'And there's a message from your cousin.'

Catherine makes a polite sound, though Rossana can tell that, as usual, she's largely indifferent. It still makes her sad. She recalls her brother's departure, years ago, on what was meant to be a brief stay; then the whales carrying news that he had fallen in love and fathered a child, then, as the years went by on both sides of the ocean, promises to hop on the next ship thwarted one after another by storms and life, until their erstwhile household had grown into two families.

Until now. It is a lovely, strange feeling to have discovered a niece – even though the young woman is not quite what Rossana expected.

They pull hard on the oars, and the first drops of rain hit them as they step on the jetty. They just have time to run to the nearest building, the transmission room of the comms centre – a low wooden affair with a turf-covered roof and surrounded by high trees turning gold, already swaying under the first breath of the storm. Rossana lifts the recorder she's taken from the boat and gestures to the woman at the screen.

'Storm warning, I think. Can we have a look?'

Outside, the rain is beginning to hammer at the university buildings, shaking the branches of the trees like musical instruments. Catherine stands at the nearby window, staring at the landscape that shifts under its curtain of moisture with an air of wonder. She's lived here all her life, yet the way she looks at the Saint-Lawrence river reminds Rossana of a little girl setting foot on a beach for the first time. It's lovely, and endearing, and it's hard to stay long near that young woman without wanting to smile.

Young people are a blessing in such times. Rossana knows that she should appreciate it unreservedly. And so she feels guilty when she thinks, as she often does, that in spite of her enthusiasm and curiosity, Catherine's wits largely lie fallow. Her years at the university were spent dawdling in the doomed byways of digital archaeology, and though Rossana has to admit that her niece is very good with computers, there is something about her, about most people in Tadoussac – academic centre as it is – that speaks of an inlander's narrow worldview, of the kind she had not expected to find next to a feeding ground bustling with news from all over the world. She doesn't like to find those thoughts in herself. She can't pretend they don't exist, though.

The comms device beeps. The woman sucks in a breath.

'You were right, Doctor Zouaoui,' she says. 'They say it's a big one. And it's heading inland. Montreal at least, maybe Toronto. We need to send warning.'

Catherine leaps to their side.

'I'll send it through the computer network. Dad says they haven't finished fixing the radio tower,' she adds, to Rossana.

The woman has left her post and is striding towards the inner rooms of the university building.

'I'll get them to initiate lockdown.' She turns around for a second at the door. 'Oh, and your son says he hopes you can meet his girlfriend when you come home. And he loves you.'

Girlfriend? Rossana is about to say. But Catherine is already pumping the pedals that get electricity flowing into the sole computer in the room.

'Can you read me the specifics of the message, Auntie?' Catherine calls.

Away from the imminence of the storm on the water, she no longer sounds tense or worried. She just sounds happy for the excuse to start the computer. Rossana sits next to her, one eye on the wavering lines that materialise the whale's message on the comms device, the other on the green shimmering letters that begin covering Catherine's screen, too fast to follow. The young woman seems entirely absorbed, then all of a sudden, without slowing down her typing, she turns to Rossana.

'I didn't know you could understand whales just by listening to them,' she says, darting quick glances at the screen. 'That's amazing!'

'I can't. I don't hear everything they say, but I can still make out some words.' Her son's name she would recognise in any language, of course. She smiles. 'And it's my job.'

'I thought your job was exploring old buildings?'

'It is. But everybody learns to speak whale in Ospedaletti.'

'Wow.'

She may sound impressed, but it is Rossana who wonders how her niece can keep pumping the pedals with such regularity while typing at that speed and holding a conversation, all without sounding even slightly out of breath. Not for the first time since the start of her sabbatical in Quebec, she marvels at how different the part of the world her brother has elected to live in is from the Riviera where they were both born. Back home, children learned to decipher greetings from passing whales as they played in the water. Here, even by the thriving feeding grounds of the Saint-Lawrence, most people only wander as far as the shore of the great cold river. But they put great stock by outdated devices, and Catherine won't stop going on about digital archaeology, which she's explored with passion, even though she had few real findings to show for it.

The sound of the pedals begins to quiet down.

'All done,' Catherine says. 'Montreal has three days to get ready. Plenty of time.'

'Are you sure they're equipped to get this? If the radio tower is broken…'

Catherine grins and rolls her eyes, Rossana is not quite sure which is supposed to mask the other.

'You can't count on computer networks alone,' she persists. Look at what happened in Europe. It took a handful of viral AIs –'

'The networks are fine, Auntie, I swear. Even inland.'

'Did you at least check…?'

Catherine kicks the pedal back with a smile that feels amused if slightly impatient.

'We check everything, all the time. Trust me.'

That will have to do. They cannot waste time agonising over how to send the message anyway; the whales don't cruise past the opening of the Saguenay River, and even their songs can't be heard far past Quebec City, so there are no more reliable ways to communicate past this point than radios and computers. The rain is building up outside, and though whales have learned over the years what humans needed to be told to protect themselves from storms, the potency of the wind is the one thing they don't quite understand or feel concerned about. This would seldom be a concern on the dry shores of the Mediterranean; but in lands of cyclones and hurricanes, every storm could, without warning, become the final one. The low, thick walls of earth and wood of the university should be safe, ensconced in their bulwark of forests. The old cities inland, however, with their ruined skyscrapers held together with vines and good luck – the remnants of a time when storms exhausted themselves long before they reached far inland – are a very different story. She goes to sleep hoping that every one of the former metropolises had someone on the other end to receive Catherine's warning.

She wakes up much sooner than she expected to.

'Doctor Zouaoui, *did you send this?*'

Rossana starts as if she had been drowning. She shields her eyes against the light the intruder has turned on, then recognises Natasha, the overseer of the comms centre. Outside, the rain is furiously pelting wood and earth.

'Did you send the warning?' Natasha repeats. 'What kind of message is this?'

Rossana sits up, beckons, rubs her eyes.

'What message? When?'

'*Miss you. Love, C.,*' Natasha replies, quoting. 'It was sent electronically to Quebec City, Trois-Rivières, Montreal and Toronto just after we started lockdown procedures. There's no word about a storm about to hit. What were you thinking?'

'Miss you? What?'

'That's all it says. Didn't you double-check?'

'I don't even know how to send these,' Rossana mutters, chewing on the words as movement returns to her face.

Her thoughts churn and she tries to grasp them. Catherine. Catherine sent the message, didn't even look at the screen after. What she had been typing had seemed much longer than the few words Natasha's just read, though Rossana had not been looking at the screen. But why on Earth would her niece do such a thing?

She doesn't bother to put proper clothes on before she jogs to the emergency dorm, where half of Tadoussac has come to wait out the storm behind thick earthen walls. She barges in, bumps into a few bunks, triggering grunts and startled exclamations. When she finds Catherine, she nearly pulls her out of bed.

'The messages! What did you do? What happened?'

Catherine rubs her eyes. When she sees the message, she covers her mouth with her hands. In the torchlight, her face turns crimson.

'It's not possible,' she says.

'Did you send this?'

'No! I mean…' Groans of protest interrupt them. They step out of the dormitory. Catherine starts towards the comms room, pulling them after her. 'I sent this three weeks ago. To… anyway, this is not what I wrote yesterday. And not what I sent, either, I swear.'

She lands on the seat with a thud and pushes on the pedals, still rubbing her face. The screen flickers alive after a while. Rossana looks at it in dismay. They sent that message nearly a day ago. They can re-send it, but how much destruction will the storm wreak because of the delay?

'I'm sorry. I'm so sorry. If this is a bug, I…'

'Why didn't you double-check?' Natasha repeats.

Catherine shakes her head, eyes down, and doesn't answer. Rossana remembers the exchange and takes her head in her hands. Her own doubts, voiced once too many, Catherine's breezy reassurances. If she had stayed silent, would Catherine have gone through her usual routine instead of acting overly confident for her benefit?

'I'm sorry,' Catherine repeats.

She works at the keyboard. She is sending the message again. Does a proper check, this time. Outside, the rain sounds like tambourines.

'There will have to be an investigation into this,' Natasha says.

It is clear, from their tone, that Catherine will be investigated more closely than the computer itself. Catherine says nothing. She is still typing, huffing with frustration every now and then. Until she freezes.

'There's something from Toronto,' she says.

The three of them rush towards the screen. It takes Rossana a while to spot the letters that make sense. It is not a response to Catherine's message.

It is a warning, and a request for help, one of a kind that Rossana had not seen for years. And yet what it warns against has shaped her youth. It was, in fact, the last lost battle in the long struggle of humankind to emerge from a collapse it had caused itself – though it had felt at the time like a skirmish, more than a battle, an exhausting fight against a mindless, invisible enemy randomly striking until most computer networks in Europe had been rendered useless. She fought in that skirmish for a time, before it was decided that the threat would only be gone once its native habitat had been destroyed, and all attempts at restoring large-scale networks on that side of the Atlantic were abandoned, ushering the old era out for good.

Except that the old era will never quite finish dying, it appears. As if the storm building up at their door was not enough – over there in the ivy jungle of Toronto, someone has spotted a rogue AI.

'Oh, porca miseria,' Rossana says before anybody else.

Catherine turns to her.

'I thought you said they'd all been wiped out?'

'I thought they had. I took down a couple myself. Well, they still destroyed most of our computer networks. Not a big deal for us, we do all right with radios, but…'

But Mediterranean storms aren't nearly as frequent or potent as the ones on this continent. Antennas don't get torn down just when you need them most. It was a blessing that nobody had been able to maintain undersea cables for decades and American networks had been able to continue in isolation. Computer networks are still a necessity here, and rogue AIs –

Rogue AIs are perfectly capable of infecting the comms network, of swallowing up all the messages still recorded and sending the ones they choose instead of the ones that were meant to arrive. As far as Rossana knows, nobody's ever really understood what went on inside an AI's pseudo-mind, not even back when they were created. *Miss you. Love, C.*

Catherine coughs tentatively.

'You do believe I didn't send that message now, don't you?' she says.

Natasha glares.

'We'll have to cut our connections to the rest of the country while we scour our servers. Inform the government. If that thing started spreading in Toronto, they'll probably have to cut the whole city off until someone's managed to locate it and clean this up – and they'll never locate it in time, with the number of unexplored buildings they have there – and they'll just have to pray storm season ends peacefully. I understand that you're concerned about what's going to happen to you, but this isn't –'

Rossana holds up her hand, suppressing a yawn.

'It's four o'clock in the morning. We're all in a foul mood. Let's save discussions for when we've had a good night's sleep, shall we?'

It sounds terrible, even as she says it. Tadoussac is a major comms centre. Nobody gets out of the responsibility of managing what goes on here; they are the only ones who can make sure that vital warnings get sent in time. It feels indecent even to mention their personal comfort, even as she yearns for her bed as if it was a loved one.

And even as she speaks she knows what she's going to say next.

'I'll go to Toronto. I've dealt with rogue AIs before. If this one is in an unexplored building, they'll need someone who knows her way around those, don't we?'

Natasha shakes her head.

'It's already interfered with our messages. I don't think there's time —'

'If I leave as soon as it's safe to, there will be. It started spreading in Toronto. That means it's probably hosted there. Send a warning now. Shut down the network, scour your hardware, and while you're doing that I'll try to find the servers it's escaped from.'

'And with a good killer script, we can make sure that it's disabled on any computer it's managed to reach,' Catherine blurts out.

Rossana and Natasha both turn to her at the same time. Catherine's face goes red.

'I mean, I'm going with you, right?' she says, her gaze pleading.

Rossana hesitates. This was not part of what she'd discussed with her brother, when she'd agreed to mentor Catherine through her next steps at the university.

'You could be useful here...' she begins.

'But even more useful with you. I've wasted us a whole day when I didn't double-check my message. And besides, we both know you're rubbish with computers.'

There's a silence. Then Natasha nods.

'Message Toronto now,' she says. 'I hope you weren't thinking of catching up on any sleep.'

Iteration #35F485AE69 – Still searching

I wanted this. I wanted you. Didn't I? I grinned when your kicks made my stomach bend outward. There's a picture to prove it, though I don't remember it being taken. I remember my body aching, however, the weight whenever I tried to stand, and longing for the day when all of this would be over, when I'd be back to what I was before you came along.

I didn't know there would be no going back. I didn't know you would scream so much. I told everyone that I'd learned the secret, that babies don't scream as long as you carry them around in a sling and shower them with love, and now I walk with you strapped to my chest, my gaze fixed straight ahead so I won't meet the stares of people around me who must be wondering why you still scream so much if I've done everything right, and I carry you; and I carry you because carrying is the only part of my plan I've managed to fulfil as yet, and I wonder if I would stop hearing your wails if I lay down and died in the middle of the road.

Two·

June, year 2 pre-disaster

'Professor Chen, it's me again, Sabrina. I may not be able to come to the lab this afternoon after all. I'm dreadfully sorry, but I'm having such trouble finding a place to stay, and this is all getting… urgh, I'm sorry. I'll try to call again and see if I can explain in person. All right, uh…'

I hung up before letting out an audible huff of frustration. I checked the number next to the door. This was the last building on my list. Warm brick façade, metallic stairs to the side – the picturesque sort I had imagined living in, but was now, after countless frigid exchanges with landlords and prospective housemates asking about my current income, beginning to think was out of my reach. The door clicked open. I took a deep breath, shoved the phone into my pocket and hurried up the stairs.

The woman who greeted me had thick black bangs, a nose ring, a sleeveless turtleneck top and the kind of devil-may-care beauty I associated with high school mean girls. She stepped aside and waved me in.

'Sabrina, right? I'm Jasminder. Let me give you the tour.'

The flat was not large, no cleaner than I'd expect from accommodation shared with a fellow post-doctoral student, and the walls were decorated with drawings of naked women entwined with flowers – Jasminder told me they were her work. I thought of the lopsided ceiling in the old town flat I shared with my mother and grandmother, angled like a cocoon, the warm terracotta tiles on the floor, relics from another time, another world, almost. This place felt… different, in every possible way. Nonetheless, I could afford the rent and there was light coming in through the bedroom window, which was more than I could say of other places I'd visited. Out of politeness, I still listened to Jasminder's explanations, while eyeing the trees outside and wondering if I would manage to sleep despite the sound of traffic.

'Feel free to bring your dates in, but if they're men, tell them to get dressed before exiting the bathroom. And if you're going to eat meat, please ventilate the kitchen. Sound fair?'

I would never have the brashness to show my mother pictures of a place where you could see the crumbs on the sofa from across the room and a woman's splayed legs in pencil pinned right above. I did like to eat meat, on occasion, and I didn't know how I'd handle sharing my living space with strangers if Jasminder felt as casual about *dates* as she let on.

I was expected to start work this very afternoon. And judging by the way my heart twisted when my eyes rested on an unmade bed, wrappers on the coffee table, all the small, messy signs of a place that was *lived in*, I knew that even my finances were only part of the problem. I needed a home. I could handle a new country; I could handle being away from the people I loved most for the first time in my existence; I couldn't handle not knowing where I would be staying by the end of the week. I glanced at the bedroom, decided that I could picture myself sleeping in there, and nodded.

'Completely fair. Can I bring my luggage in?'

She raised an eyebrow. I gave an inward sigh, knowing what was coming.

'I still have a couple of people to interview,' she began. 'I suppose I'll call you...?'

She paused in surprise. I realised I must have visibly slumped. She looked at me for a few moments.

'Where did you say you were from again?'

'Italy. This is my first post-doc. I mean, I hope.'

I forced out a laugh to pretend that I meant that as a joke. I was about to get sacked from a life-changing job because I was too busy trying not to be homeless to show up on my first day; my new life would end before it had even begun, but it seemed pointless to say that out loud, or worse, ungracious. My face must have shown something, however. Jasminder looked taken aback.

Then she shrugged.

'You know what – go ahead. I've had it with interviews anyway. Living with a stranger or living with a stranger, same difference. You sound all right.'

I clapped my hands over my mouth and a squeal escaped before I could help it.

'You've just saved my life. I was going to be homeless and jobless and I have just barely enough to take the plane back, my God... Thank you!'

22

She smiled, eyebrows still raised. I'd read in her ad that she worked in research too; but it was clear, from her demeanour, that the predicament of her more indigent peers wasn't much more than a theoretical reality for her. She waved around.

'Welcome home, then. What do you work on, by the way?'

I was so relieved I let my shoulders sag and dropped the bag I had been holding to the floor. I beamed at her.

'New models of machine learning. Professor Chen – he's the one who won that Nobel three years ago – his lab has this cutting-edge tech they're using, and they've just hired me on the project, I'm so excited…' Jasminder's face had frozen. I trailed off.

'Machine learning. Huh.' She still looked carefully blank for a moment, then shrugged. 'Well, I'm not enough of a jerk to tell you to pack up your things at that point. You best remember I'm opting *the fuck* out of that "cutting-edge tech," though. Oh, and you'll need to bring the deposit in cash.'

Her bedroom door made a too-loud sound when she closed it behind her.

THREE

September, year 164 post-disaster

Rossana is not used to silent waters. Though the familiar whirring of the wind turbine and the low rumble of the electric motor are in the background, she notices herself straining to hear clacking sounds in the water and faraway whistles, ubiquitous as they are in the open sea and near her home. But this far upriver, where even dolphins are no longer comfortable swimming, whale songs only travel as unreadable echoes, bounced back and muddled in the silt. Though, ahead, the flat horizon and lapping waves look like the sea, there is no mistaking the open lake they are entering, the sweet smell of inland water and the intermittent buzzing of the comms apparatus. Rossana stands at the prow, tuning her ears and skin and nose to the new voices that wander with the wind, the songs of unfamiliar birds and scents of new earths freshly disturbed by the receding storm. She wonders what the famous ivy skyline, the first regrown city in the world if records have it right, will look like from the lake.

Footsteps behind her break the quiet, and her focus. She glances back. Catherine walks briskly towards her, beaming and waving a piece of paper. Rossana smiles. For the first time in a while, standing on the deck of a ship and attuning herself to a new environment, part of her feels at home; and though Catherine grew up on a different continent, she feels that the two of them share a bond that bypasses cultural distance. *Ragazze della città e del mare*, as they say back home; *min el-bahr wa-l-medina* – women of the comms centres, the two of them, grown between the worlds of humans and whales.

'Radio message for you, Doctor Zouaoui,' Catherine says, handing out the paper with a mock salute.

'Already?'

Catherine raises an uncertain eyebrow.

'Why, yes,' she says. 'This is a backwater, not the end of the world.'

Rossana laughs. The message is succinct. And it still uses the old Christian dating system rather than the one adopted after the world was turned upside down.

'Fair enough. Well, would you look at that: *Confirmed localisation of rogue AI. Ivy strain unknown.*' She reads the rest quickly, folds the paper back up, and smiles, saying, 'It seems I'm indeed taking you on your first exploration mission.'

Catherine whoops and claps her hands on the railing.

'The ivy skyscrapers. I can't believe it!' She squints, but there is no seeing past the horizon yet. 'They must have all sorts of data left in there. Just imagine, if they had desktop computers in secure chambers, and the ivy didn't get in…'

'I hardly think we'll have time to hunt for old desktops,' Rossana says, gentle but final.

Catherine abruptly falls silent. Rossana immediately regrets being so blunt. Though Natasha agreed to let

25

Catherine go, the flares of raised voice through the door in the morning told Rossana that the dressing-down had been forceful. And here she is now, rebuking her again for her love of ancient computers. She pats her back.

'You're bound to dig through a few computers as we search for this rogue AI,' she says. 'But I hope you're not counting on spending too long over it. And I wouldn't hope too much about the ivy. It's an old engineered strain they have over there. Quite uncontrolled, I should think. It probably punched holes through every wall it could reach.'

Catherine nods with a tight-lipped smile.

'I'll go review our gear before we land,' she says, and leaves.

Rossana watches her go with a small pang. Young people. She misses her son. She had hoped to get another message from him right until the ship sailed past the clump of islands ahead of Québec City; even after that, she listened for the pattern of his name in the jumbled echoes, and consoled herself by telling Catherine stories of his childhood. The saying is right: a thousand kilometres inland is a greater distance between two humans than an entire ocean. Every perception here is a reminder of the fresh water around her, the air currents from the far north, the young regrown forests – so unlike the thriving areas around the marine comms centres in Tadoussac, Ushuaia or Ospedaletti, and their waters, teeming with whale pods guiding returning ships to safety and passing on news from everywhere in the world in exchange for a crate of fresh fish. It's easy to forget at times that the rest of the world has not been completely returned to the wilderness.

She turns her gaze ahead. Pleased as she is to conduct exploration work again, she doesn't expect an easy task. Engineered ivy can be full of unforeseen dangers, and who knows how they will have to negotiate with inlanders when it comes to making decisions about the mission? Catherine can deal with a little disappointment; it's not like her years in digital archaeology have been filled with productive work, anyway. There is enough to do.

Not long after, the giant kite-sail tethered to the bow unfurls with a great flap and stabilises in the wind thirty metres above them, and the ship glides on the mirror-grey expanse towards the setting sun.

Iteration #3612A57C – Still searching

Summer, family gathered in the shade of the parasol, the scent of Granny's cooking – memories over gastronomy, but I'm wolfing it down nonetheless – chomping on a piece of stewed meat and swallowing while you all chatter and laugh – when time freezes.

I can't swallow. Or breathe. I gape, reach with my fingers to the bottom of my mouth. Someone comments on my table manners. You all laugh. I try to shout for help but there's no air so I only gesture, stand wildly, my chair flying back; you all keep looking and laughing and not even in my nightmares have people I loved watched me DIE with laughter on their faces but you still don't understand –

Until someone's laugh falters, then another's. Someone asks if I'm all right. Of course there's no answer, and then time begins flying again. The shouts that I couldn't push out exit other people's mouths. Someone bends me over, slams their hand against my back, one two three f…

I gurgle and spit out half-chewed meat and the contents of my stomach, and collapse to my knees, my body out of control, snot and tears and high-pitched sounds coming out, but the air is coming back it and God I'm so terrified I was about to die and I cannot answer questions only weep and shake and thank God I am still alive.

FOUR

June, year 2 pre-disaster

I had a brief pang when I heard my mother's voice through the phone that morning, six time zones away. I hadn't seen her face since she dropped me off at the airport, smiling too hard so she wouldn't start crying and arguing with my grandmother who didn't bother to pretend that my departure made her happy. That had been three days before – far longer than I'd ever spent without seeing her, and I was farther away than I'd ever been from her. I'd rehearsed what I would tell her even before I'd found a place to stay: yes, the bedroom is large enough, no, there is no chance of my flatmate throwing me out on a whim, yes, I've filled the fridge with enough vegetables and meat to tide me over to Christmas. I could hear that she was at work, taking a break before going back to the dead-white limbo of the supermarket – a place where, she often joked, you at least found air conditioning if not common decency.

'Nonna tells you she's still waiting for you to make her that android you promised,' she said, the warmth in her voice too thin to hide her tiredness.

The smile froze on my face. I knew she hadn't meant to remind me, but my grandmother was still waiting for an assigned nurse to take care of her when my mother was at work. And I was no longer there to help.

I hung up before it grew too tempting to tell her how much I already missed them.

I was out of the door without having talked to anyone else. Jasminder had been in the kitchen when I grabbed my breakfast, talking on the phone in angry tones about an editor who had refused to pay her what her art was worth, or something of the kind. I'd almost asked about it when she'd hung up, but then she'd glanced my way with a very blank face, grunted something vague and headed out without a word before I finished eating. I hopped on a bike from the nearest outpost, and zig-zagged between enormous cars and construction sites, towards the buildings of the university. The hot summer air slapping my hair against my face soon dispelled my lingering gloom.

I only got lost for a few minutes before I managed to find my mentor's office, somewhere at the bottom of a long windowless corridor.

'How is your installation going?' Professor Chen asked, walking me to the lab with no more ado.

A hundred answers wanted to tumble out of my mouth at the same time: how heat was the last thing I'd expected to suffer from when leaving Italy for Canada, but damp Ontarian summers were even more oppressive than the dog days back home – how, after leaving a hopelessly ageing, derelict economy, everything here felt like youth, and wealth – how Canadian coffee tasted like strong tea at best, but also like the unbelievable luxury of having a job, and my own salary – how I had left a town of stone and red tiles for one of concrete and glass, vertical lines towering so high you could wonder how humans had managed to create them, and where every time I found myself outside, the city would assault my eyes from all directions at once, students racing through mud-thick traffic on rented bikes, the construction sites along the road, the imposing outlines of the university's buildings, the skyscrapers behind like mirrors, all too large, too gleaming, yet somehow the sun came in from everywhere, and I could always find maple trees to rest my eyes on.

But Professor Chen had far better things to do than listen to my ramblings, as eagerly as I might have wanted to share them with someone.

'All good,' I said instead, and grinned. My surly flatmate aside, I still felt the giddiness of a new chapter opening. 'New city, new life!'

Though my mentor smiled, he raised a polite eyebrow. 'Postdocs are not meant to have *lives*,' he said, in a tone which might have been playful. 'I am pleased that you got accommodation sorted out quickly, though. Let's take a look at the project, shall we?'

The rest of the day was a whirlwind of handshakes and attempting to remember names. Suitably haggard PhD students greeted me with something like awe, while fellow postdocs, their desks littered with coffee cups, sandwich wrappers and printed-out graphs, waved from behind their screens and then launched into rapid-fire summaries of their data, too quickly for me to process at once.

'This one here is from when we managed to predict chimpanzee behaviour from their brainwaves,' a young

Arab woman with thick tousled hair said, tracing patterns on the screen. 'The one that got the Nobel Prize. Yep, I was already here,' she added, with a laugh that could have reflected pride, exhaustion, or disbelief. 'Pretty useful to know when to duck because you're about to get pelted with cucumber bits. I mean, I think.'

'And it works on humans?'

She glanced over her screen, then leaned towards me and lowered her voice. 'I'm still not sure it really works on chimps, to be honest. We can tell when they're about to act out. We still can't tell why, and I'm not sure how much anyone cares. But hey –' Chen suddenly appeared in the doorway, and she dropped her voice to a whisper, which did not keep away her mirth, 'for the kind of grant money I got, I'm happy doing anything he tells me to. Even if these days it's mostly writing requests for more funding and orders for state-of-the-art hard drives. His Professorial Magnificence wants our data to last for the next century at least, you see.'

She took a gulp from her mug. It bore the logo of a biology lab, and had a pod of killer whales on it. In delight, I instantly dropped the conversation we'd been having.

'I used to volunteer for a charity that taught people how to keep whales safe while sailing,' I said. 'Did you work on –?'

'I'm going to borrow Sabrina for a couple of hours,' Chen's voice cut in.

His booming address sent a wave of reverent silence across the lab – myself included. I shot up, gave the other girl a quick wave and practically ran to heel. I had just lifted myself out of my post-defence slump, and I was already chatting with a Nobel Prize winner, one who was about to turn the tide of what artificial intelligence could do for humankind, no less. Chimps, he'd explained to me, had only been a first step; his current ambitions would have much more dramatic implications for the world I knew. Translating the brain waves of humans into a coherent account of the emotions they were experiencing, consciously or not – a revolution for medicine, mental health, and, Chen hoped, for the field of artificial intelligence at large; once machines could suss out how humans felt, the concept of an empathetic, benevolent artificial consciousness would not be far behind. I followed, asking questions I knew I would never manage to remember the answers to, excitement bubbling over wisdom.

It was only after some time that my earlier conversation with Jasminder came back to my mind. I tentatively mentioned it when I ran out of immediate questions. Professor Chen sighed.

'This is an expensive project, as you can imagine. And so, by necessity, an unpopular one. Between you and me, I regret some of the sponsors we have to work with, I truly do. But what else can be done today?'

I nodded, not quite knowing how else to react. Universities got their funding where the money was, it was a fact of life, as were the accompanying controversies, given that nearly all public research was funded by private sponsors. The same wealth that was busy overthrowing democracies the world over extended a generous hand to research, and very few labs could afford to turn it down. Back home, the joke went that as long as you could avoid mafia money or billionaires with sex-trafficking convictions, you could pride yourself on ethical funding. Being unhappy with how reality worked did not make it less real, I reasoned.

'I hold that ethics apply to what we choose to do with our research, not what grants we are forced to accept,' Professor Chen went on. 'If we can get machines to understand human emotions, we may get them to understand once and for all why there is so much resistance to tackling climate change, among other things.'

He smiled at that. I nodded again, with more enthusiasm. Working on computer models of climate change – my personal compromise, when my studies had become too demanding to keep up with volunteer work – was what had got me this job in the first place. I thought of my grandmother hanging damp curtains across windows during summer heatwaves when money was too scarce for air conditioning. Then I thought of my new home, and of one last detail I'd wanted to clarify.

'My housemate also said something about "opting out"?'

I hadn't even managed to ask her what exactly she'd meant. Professor Chen stopped smiling.

'We use non-invasive sensors to record brain waves at a distance,' he said. 'We are forced to restrict usage to labs that haven't transmitted an explicit opt-out request. Given the sheer volume of data this project requires, this is a great inconvenience. And one I can hardly sympathise with, seeing as we gather no identifying materials whatsoever.' He laid a hand on my shoulder. 'Don't let yourself get dragged into political squabbles, Sabrina. You have a career to focus on.'

Five

September, year 164 post-disaster

Rossana and Catherine stay up late. Reading by the light of a storm lamp, they go through a heap of articles on genetically altered plants from the early post-disaster age – a huge file that Catherine assembled in a hurry before they left, which they haven't yet had time to read in full. Catherine's focus is dwindling, but Rossana still pushes a few pages her way.

'Take a look at this. Miami, before the levees broke. They used bio-engineered ivy to prevent a few skyscrapers from falling down, during late collapse times. Pioneering work, shortly after Toronto. But they had too little time to test it properly, and it was this very ivy that escaped and destroyed some nearby swamp ecosystems –'

'Why are we looking at this, exactly?' Catherine says, catching another yawn.

Rossana frowns.

'The AI isn't everything,' she says. 'Since we're going to do this, we need clues about the identity of the Toronto strain. What to watch out for when we explore the buildings. And whether it might pose a danger to nearby forests, and we'll have to call the government for intervention.'

'They've been managing just fine on their own so far,' Catherine says.

'So far, yes. But inlanders have their own way to manage, believe me. Stewardship doesn't enter into it.'

The word slipped from her tongue before she could think better of it. *Inlander* is what children from Ospedaletti call each other before they understand the difference between a joke and an insult, and what some adults mutter, less pleasantly, whenever they confront a display of ignorance or close-mindedness. Rossana wishes she found it entirely unjustified. She can't help being angry, however, whenever she hears reports of inland populations cutting down forests or diverting rivers for quick convenience. Catherine rubs her eyes, then when she notices Rossana's gaze, she tries to smile.

'You know, I'm sure we'd have found plenty of data in those recovered servers, if you'd let me take a couple. Disaster-era stuff. I'm sure the hard drives would have been in decent condition.'

Rossana shakes her head, smiling. Trust Catherine to be unable to let go of her old obsessions, even when going on the biggest mission of her career so far.

'And how long would it take you to make sense of it? We have everything we need here. We'll find out the rest when we explore the building.' She pats Catherine's hand. 'Go get some sleep.'

Catherine nods, a deflated look on her face, but still clears their small table before curling up on her bunk. The gentle flapping of the kite-sail lulls them to sleep.

The dawn wakes Rossana, and when she notices the empty bunk below her she climbs up to the deck, invigorated at the thought of the day to come. Catherine is already there, griping the railing and staring.

'Oh my God, Auntie. I was just about to wake you up. I've been wanting to talk to someone since first light. This is incredible.'

She points at the jagged horizon, waters still grey in the rising light, and Rossana stares in turn.

Unknown strains or not, it *is* beautiful. The land rises over the lake in a softly shifting array, a bloom of light and dark green, with the glint of broken window panes in places where the old façades show through the ivy that has covered the entire city, dwarfing the red and gold expanse of maple trees at its feet. The oldest bio-architectural ensemble in the world, she's always been told, quietly tucked behind a lake, just a couple of rivers away from being truly lost at the end of the world as the alliance between humans and whales remade it. The buildings, she heard, are still amazingly whole under their covering of vines. Even the needle of the radio tower still soars tall, like a beanstalk thrusting upwards.

The harbour itself is across a small, intimate bay, with no space for larger ships or visiting whales. Tendrils of ivy break up the pavement here and there; a goat looks askance at a herd of geese and a flock of seagulls bickering over the side of the road. A man holds a cardboard sign up high, with Rossana's name written on it. He waves. Shortly after, Rossana feels solid ground under her feet once more.

'We're lucky you could make it,' the man says.

Rossana takes his proffered hand. He's a few years older than her son, a bit taller, his skin a shade darker, and his expression has something of the dourness she associates with inlanders. She smiles and glances around, shaking the chill out of her limbs. Long as the journey was, she feels invigorated, not weary. It has been a long time – since her own post-doctoral studies, in fact – since she was involved in actual exploration work, though this remains what she is renowned for. Around her native Ospedaletti, bio-architectural structures have all been consolidated or returned to the wild, and there has been no need for new exploration in years.

Catherine comes to stand at her side, expectant. Rossana pats her shoulder.

'My niece, Catherine Vigneault. Our best computer wizard,' she says.

'I'm a digital archaeologist,' Catherine cuts in, beaming at the man – Ishmael, they will learn later – but not before casting a pointed glance at Rossana, who waves her objection away. Then she rushes to help the sailors unload their equipment, cameras and measuring devices, and Catherine's beloved computer paraphernalia. There are bikes at the ready, and they set out along the avenue, weaving between reclaimed fields where the roadway used to be, bumping over roots and remnants of broken-down asphalt and gazing around at the uncanny majesty of the ivy towers, massive, yet with enough space between them to let the sun in.

Once or twice, Rossana looks up to gaze at the strange architecture surrounding them. Tall, vertical lines: very different from the stucco-laden majesty of the Riviera's ancient buildings or from the earth-and-wood buildings of the modern comms centres. An in-between city, soaring concrete and glass, one meant for a future that heatwaves and storms engulfed before it could happen.

'So, rogue AI?' Catherine calls over the sound of the wheels.

Ishmael veers around a pumpkin patch and makes a sound between a chuckle and a sigh.

'Amazing how these keep popping up out of nowhere, isn't it?' he says. Then he grows more serious. 'This one is better-preserved than usual, however.'

On the side of the road, two people carry a heavy wooden beam. The building at the corner has a ruined roof and a couple of broken windows.

'Did the storm hurt anyone?' Catherine asks.

Ishmael pinches his lips.

'Not this time, no. We couldn't protect the buildings with so little advance warning, though. We hunkered down and hoped for the best.' He shruggs. 'Don't we all?'

Catherine looks straight ahead, face immobile. Rossana picks up the pace and gives her what she hopes is a reassuring nod. Ishmael says nothing more, though, and she decides never to tell him that his city could have received the warning almost a day earlier.

'That AI,' she says. 'How did you find out about it?'

'We came across some unusual comms a few days ago. We attempted to track it down, but its firewall holds strong. It's an active one, though, and enthusiastic. We messaged you as soon as we were sure, but it's emerging fast. Since you set out, we've already found parasitic text in several transmitted messages.'

'I'm sorry,' Catherine says.

But Ishmael shakes his head, pleasantly.

'No need for that. What matters now is to save our link with marine comms.'

Catherine frowns.

'I still don't understand. How could an AI tamper with whale song? It couldn't even make sense of it!'

'Picking up on whatever human speech patterns whales have learned to mimic, I assume,' Ishmael replies, and shrugs. 'I wouldn't know. I don't know much about how marine comms work. You can tell us. We're very lucky you were available,' he adds with a tentative smile in Rossana's direction.

She acknowledges his deference with a non-committal nod.

'I'm staying in Tadoussac for the year. This is the least I could do.'

'Well, so much the better for us. We heard about your work. A couple of old skyscrapers here were recovered thanks to your methods. Though I hear your articles make it sound easier than it actually is,' he adds, still smiling.

She chuckles. She doesn't recall writing anything anywhere to the effect that exploration was *easy*. She learned to understand ecosystems the way potters learn to centre a lump of clay on the wheel at the first try: an attuning of the body, a process words cannot account for except by making it sound *easier than it actually is*. She doubts Ishmael would understand. She grew up by the sea, attuning her ears to whale song even as communicators deciphered their patterns to retrieve the messages they carried; he has probably never heard the language of another species, except in translation, in the forecasts the comms centres send when a storm threatens to hit, or the news from across the world whales carry over the ocean and wire networks take inland. Her mind circles back to the rogue AI. Ishmael is right to be worried.

'It's good that you reacted so quickly,' she said. 'We could recover an infected communicator, but if we had to permanently disconnect the devices from the network…'

He nods. Bad news for anyone not living near a comms centre, or at least a port city. A place like Toronto could sink into destitution overnight if it found itself unprepared in the way of a storm.

Rossana pushes hard on the pedals, trying to shake off a baseless feeling of dread. Artificial *intelligence* was never more than a brag; true malevolence is beyond its scope. Only, in their mindlessness, such tools were (are still) scarily effective at what they were built for: stealthily accessing systems to filter their content and then selecting relevance by popularity, amplifying some messages and suppressing others to the point of making original outputs unrecognisable. Stories still go around of ships being sunk and buildings being destroyed, after rogue AIs infiltrated communications and delivered the messages they considered most likely to please humans, rather than the ones that were meant to arrive. Legends are born with less, and in Ospedaletti, people use another word for rogue AIs, jokingly but also not quite. *Ghosts.*

'Are you positive about the location?' she asks.

'We've already combed through every alternative. It must be inside the museum. It's completely overgrown in there, some floors have fallen, and the walls are angled wrong. Nothing you won't be able to handle,' Ishmael adds with a slightly forced grin.

She smiles back, tightly. Ishmael points ahead, at a mass of greenery that seems to lean over the street. Catherine sucks in a breath.

'Everything's all right?' Rossana asks.

'This couldn't get cooler if you told me we were going to the moon,' Catherine replies.

Finally they dismount. Two other people are waiting in front of a gap in the vines. Rossana reviews the supplies they've brought, thanking them: dense lentil and honey cakes, strips of dried meat, hand-cranked batteries, bedrolls – looking at the size of the building, they will need two or three days to fine-comb every corner for the kind of electronics that could hold the source code for a rogue AI, and, from Ishmael's account, the matter is too urgent to spread their search over several trips. Then, backpacks and harnesses secure about their bodies, they stand across the threshold. It's pitch dark inside, and, misgivings or not, Rossana can't help smiling.

It's a brand-new world they're about to enter.

Iteration #37568FAC – Still searching

I thought I'd recognise everything. The corner where you splashed wine and we never really managed to scrub the stain. The dirt falling from pots on the balcony. The lulling softness of the bedroom.

But for the layout of the walls, nothing of what used to be our life remains. I force myself to smile as the new owners tell me of things they call 'improvements'. They've been diligent indeed. But why shouldn't they? We chose to sell this place, after all. I already knew the kitchen we'd built was not to their taste.

I didn't expect this sorrow at no longer seeing the traces of us. I glance your way, and see it on your face, too. We shouldn't have come back here. Let memories lie without painting them over with sadness.

Coffee, pleasantries, and we're gone as soon as politeness allows.

Six

November, year 2 pre-disaster

The lab was silent. As often happened, I'd won the tacit game of one-upmanship between postdocs ostensibly overworking themselves, and stayed later than anyone else. I dared a brief video call with my mother, gushed about how well everything was going, swore that I would be able to take a day off for Christmas Eve and join her and Nonna on video for dinner, and even managed to believe in my own words – at least until the call ended, and I faced the output from the AI again.

I slumped over my desk, head in my hands and coffee thrumming in my temples. It was dark outside, had been for a long while. The noise from the construction sites on the street had died down at last. When I looked back at the screen, its light flickered and I squinted, the glare too much to bear for more than a brief while.

A few blinks later, the words displayed there were still hopelessly jumbled. I switched tabs and stared at the incomprehensible pattern of brain waves. The program could no more make sense of it than I did. I switched back to the latest article Professor Chen had sent me, a gushing expose on the preliminary results my predecessor had

44

obtained, before their contract ended and they disappeared into the wild.

I skimmed over the results, too tired to check the maths again. In response to the brain waves, and after painstakingly connecting limited numbers of keywords to their patterns and letting the program draw what conclusions it would, the machine had indeed produced words in response to new input, in a pattern that had clearly not been random – or so the paper said. From there to translating recorded brain waves into identifiable emotions was only a matter of time, or so Professor Chen had told me, with a confidence that would have convinced a stronger woman than me. In the meanwhile, I had been unable to replicate even the faintest correlation from my predecessor's article. The machine might as well have selected words with a throw of dice.

'Was "time" supposed to mean "decades"?' I muttered.

I stood up. It was past nine o'clock, I had made no progress in months, despite yet another preliminary paper my mentor had insisted we send out. The corridors of the university were silent. I wondered if the sensors of the recording machine were still turned on. I wondered if they would record my own brain waves, and whether someone, years later, would run a random sample through the computer and read the story of a dejected post-doctoral fellow whose body could hardly remember what time or what season it was.

And with that, I felt my mind wake up again.

I had been about to walk out. Instead, I slammed my laptop shut and ran into the next room, the one where a tall, nondescript white box stood against the wall in a mess of dusty wires, surrounded by computer screens and a single gurney – according to Chen, a deliberately dismal look for his most vital piece of equipment. Some students had once tried to find and destroy the sensors he used to sample the brain waves of passers-by (or maybe they hadn't, but Chen thought they eventually might; I'd never been able to ascertain which), and he had decided that allowing the place to look like an abandoned storage room would throw them off the scent, if they ever got past the locked doors. I'd been sceptical, but his theories about how students' minds worked had never seemed worth questioning. I kicked a cardboard box out of the way, pressed a few buttons, and waited for the recording apparatus to whir back to life, staring at the white box throughout.

The noise when I opened my own laptop woke something up in me, something not even caffeine had managed to touch in a while. I waited a few moments for the recording of my brainwaves to be completed. My own mind, laid flat in ones and zeroes. I knew for a fact it was nobody else's; getting AI to tease apart the brainwaves of the dozen strangers who walked past the machine every day had been Chen's last major achievement; and anyway, nobody ever walked past the lab at this hour. I still did not feel I could fully comprehend how that happened, my thoughts jumping into a machine without so much as an electrode touching my scalp, without feeling a single thing. A brief, unwelcome thought of Jasminder and her insistence on opting out intruded, before I pushed it away. I uploaded the input, typed a few extra lines of code, and –

Hope. And excitement. I don't know if this is going to work but at least this is me doing something, *not moving in circles. Feeling very strange about this but what if Chen had completely missed the point when he described sample emotions with isolated keywords, not complex discourse and context? Emotions are complex things, aren't they? I mean, at this point I'm starting to wonder if Chen has experienced emotions at all in his life, and I feel guilty about this because I trust him and he's so much smarter than I am and also I owe him my job, but he freaks me out sometimes. Anyway, it's the weirdest thing but I feel pretty sure he's been wrong all this time.*

I can't help imagining how thrilled I'll be if this works. I'm terrified it won't. Please let this be an intelligent idea.

I hope all the coffee I drank won't fuck the recording up.

Input. No output. The sample, and the words I'd just attached to it, disappeared into the depths of the database and left me alone, to face a room that was exactly the same as before.

I closed my eyes and tried not to doubt. Only when I'd managed to let my mind drift for a couple of minutes did I turn the recording on again.

This time I began to type my description while the machine ran.

I'm not that eager to go home. I'd look for a new place if I could be bothered. I've disliked Jasminder from the start, and it was a mistake to think that wouldn't be a problem. My family is six time zones away, I have no life to speak of and I feel even more alone than if I was truly alone. Oh, and I wish she'd tell her *dates to put something on before they leave the bathroom. Just because they're girls doesn't mean I want to know what style of knickers they prefer. God, it feels so mean-spirited to type this. But also cathartic. Fuck my flatmate.*

I was beginning to giggle. I turned the recording off. Loaded the sample. Input. No output.

'Let's see if you can digest that, you artificial stupid you,' I said.

I grinned. I wasn't feeling sleepy any longer.

I was going to need more coffee.

SEVEN

It is not quite dark inside the museum. The masonry has crumbled around several windows, allowing sunlight in – and letting the vines grow around the floors, strengthening the structure with their web.

Rossana gives the safety lines around her companions' waists a good tug, then surreptitiously, bends to check Catherine's harness one last time. Her niece's first exploration – she can't be too careful.

'The plants were engineered to hold the floors together,' she says. 'Most of the structure will be sound. But don't forget that these are living organisms, and ones that are designed for adaptability under stress. In most buildings I've studied, the ivy had evolved stronger roots and punched holes into floors and walls. It couldn't have survived in the dark.' She lifts a hanging branch and watches it ripple towards the ceiling. 'Seeing how it has thrived in here, I'm guessing that this strain has adapted. Watch your step and stay on the thicker branches if you can. And don't use the machete unless you're utterly stuck. The whole plant can feel the damage, and you never know how fast some strains can regrow when they're attacked.

We could lose our way if there's significant new growth by the time we come back here.'

She then motions them to silence. The various devices she's brought are adjusting, taking stock of the wavelengths of light and the inaudible vibrations coursing through the floor, but the device she most needs is herself, and she opens up in the quiet.

Light – patches of green and gold, letting her know where the holes in the floors might be and how they snake up to the top.

Scents: damp stone and the characteristic notes of rot, where walls are being converted into soil.

Sounds: water dripping, creatures scurrying. So the museum is no longer dormant. It's come alive; and as for humans, they are now guests here, petitioning for the right to tread on its grounds.

She catches Ishmael's arm when he wobbles on the uneven stairs. He steadies himself with a chuckle.

'Good thing we brought you in,' he says again.

She makes a vague sound of thanks and points him to the place where thick branches with fur-like bark have secured the floor tiles in place. She keeps watching until he finds his bearings.

'First time explorer?' she asks, trying not to make it sound condescending.

'More or less. I'm with the farmland reclamation team. We've been through sewers, collapsed houses, that sort of thing. Nothing this large, though. Usually the best way to find usable soil is just to clear-cut overgrown gardens.' This last is said with what feels to her like a wary glance.

She retains a carefully blank face. *Inlanders*, she catches herself thinking. Still fighting the old, long-lost war between farms and forests. Something of her disapproval must have shown, however. He pinches his lips.

'I'm raising a daughter on a maple grove, myself. But we can't survive on maple sugar alone.'

Catherine suddenly wedges herself between the two of them.

'I grew up in a maple shack!' she says, flashing Ishmael her friendliest expression. 'Snuck out to drink the sap straight from the bucket in the spring. Does your daughter do that, too?'

She listens to his answer with delight, only turning to give Rossana a stern glance when he isn't looking. Rossana takes the rebuke in her stride. Catherine is right, of course; the next couple of days will be very long indeed if they set off on the wrong footing.

'So how come nobody has explored this place before?' she says.

'You'll laugh me out of the party if I tell you.'

She raises an eyebrow. He snorts, a bit sheepishly.

'All right. Some kids went in on a dare, a few years ago. They thought the architecture would be as predictable as the skyscrapers by the waterfront. They got lost, two of them ended up falling through a crack somewhere. It must have been really overgrown, because no one ever managed to recover them. After that, and stories the third kid told… let's just say this place gives everybody the creeps. Kid swore ghosts came at them while they were trying to get out.'

Rossana is careful not to smile too broadly, given what Ishmael said about sounding ridiculous.

'In Italy, "ghosts" are what people call rogue AIs,' she says.

'Perhaps. Rogue AIs don't get into your head, though.'

They've reached the top of the stairs. Catherine delicately parts a curtain of ivy with the tip of her machete, then secures it in a bundle with loosely wrapped twine. Rossana hides a smile, and makes a note of telling her brother how easily his daughter remembered her instructions, when they come back. There's a door crumbling in its frame right behind, a hollow in the floor they carefully circle, then a tougher partition of wood they have to join forces to pull to the side, sending insects racing to the ceiling –

Then Rossana jumps back with a cry before the monster crashes down on her.

Catherine catches her just before she tangles her feet in the ivy and falls backwards. Ishmael sucks in a breath and freezes, then the three of them stare down at the remnants of the creature that has shattered in the place where Rossana was standing a moment before. Protruding bones, a sail-like ridge on its back, jaws like a serrated vice. White plaster showing in the places where the monster broke.

Catherine's shaky laughter breaks the moment at last.

'I thought it was alive!'

Rossana kneels down. A detached piece of the cast, cushioned in the net of branches on the ground, splits in two at her touch, though she still has time to recognise it: the skeleton of a dimetrodon, large as a wolf, which growing strands of ivy had lifted from its stand. She remembers another encounter, years ago: a lynx lurking in one of the regrown hotels of Sanremo, and a face-off that had lasted for the longest moments of her life; the cat growling at her and squatting as if to pounce, her lifting the flaps of her coat to intimidate it with size she didn't possess and praying to God that the beast would find an escape route other than over her mauled body.

Catherine joins them at last.

'It feels like stepping back in time,' she whispers.

Rossana beams her torch inward. The hall that stretches ahead is almost entirely overgrown. She recognises strands from a first growth, hanging down but dead and dried now, overgrown with new ivy, its dented leaves small and dark. Like the forest floor, light-deprived, but rich enough in water and loam that it feeds the creepers in their long quest towards the light.

More of the ancient monsters are peeking through the green. The sight is arresting, millions of years compressed in the deceptive quiet of a living crypt. Resin models of synapsids lie half-tumbled, propped on remnants of pedestals wrapped in dark wood. Rossana would have thought herself unafraid of wild beasts. Growing up in Ospedaletti, she learned to talk to whales almost as soon as she'd learned to talk to humans, reaching out to them in sailboats and trading fish and a moment of companionship for news from across the world, reports on fish stocks and, above all, early warnings of coming storms, the knowledge of which had allowed life in port cities to exist and thrive again. But these primitive beasts wake something in her, disquiet and yearning mingled, the awareness of time vanishing and crushing at the same time.

The museum must have lain unexplored for generations. Rossana's heart speeds up. She wonders if old-time Egyptologists felt the same way, entering the tombs of the old kings and thinking of riches and curses. A sudden sadness wells up, when she remembers that, like Egyptologists entering tombs only to cart their contents away into museums, they could be the first and last to see the building in this state. Invasive ivy (if this is what this strain turns out to be) must be destroyed; a heartbreaking loss to prevent much greater damage.

They still have to face the monsters, however. She walks forward, feeling for cracks in the floor.

Iteration #4A2865B1 – Still searching

Late spring, sunlight, just warm enough to be perfectly comfortable outdoors. I could spend the whole day sitting here, on that park bench with the river bubbling ahead, flowers competing for my attention all around. But the book I've just closed is where my mind lingers.

I don't know why something tightens in my throat and my stomach, why I can't stop thinking about it. A man in the service of a dictator, half demon and half angel, the redemption of love cut short by an ignominious death. Springtime caresses my skin, but all I want is to reach out through reality itself, and find that man and rescue him from that jail before he dies. Maybe after that the world will be beautiful and there will be no more dictators and love will truly conquer everything, and it will be springtime forever and I will be able to reach out and touch whatever it is that the tightening in my throat urges me to have, and I will no longer feel it aching.

EiGHt

March, year 1 pre-disaster

Professor Chen dumped a folder on my desk just as I was about to leave.

'Good job, Sabrina. The journal wants your paper. Give me those additional stats they request by noon tomorrow, will you?'

I stared at him and eventually forced a smile out. Publication credit. Good. God, I was bone-tired.

'Tomorrow noon. Got it.'

My mentor grinned.

'See? I told you it would interest consumer research. You're doing well, Sabrina.'

It was almost nine o'clock and the only thing I could still think about was how on Earth Chen could still manage such a sprightly gait as he walked around the lab at that hour. I waited until he'd walked through the door again, humming to himself, and then slumped backwards in my chair. Too late, I realised that I still hadn't told him about my decision to feed the machine with my own input. The more I put it off, the more difficult it became to explain. I'd initially wondered if he would disapprove; now I was quite certain he would. Unless the new data was swallowed whole and never had a chance to teach the program anything, it might invalidate much of the very article I was supposed to be working on. That meant one less line on my résumé, several months of work lost to the aether, all thanks to a sudden flare of scientific integrity.

Maybe it had not been such a bad idea to stay silent then, at least until I had some kind of proof that my idea was going to work.

By the time I got home, I'd drunk two more cups of coffee, my head was too full of numbers to sleep, and as I got into the kitchen for a snack, I met the raised eyebrows of a dark-haired White girl lounging at the table in a pair of shorts.

'Oh. Um. Hi. I'm Jasminder's flatmate,' I muttered, wondering why I felt the need to justify my presence to this stranger. Briefly, my eyes flickered above her head to the piece of paper pinned to the wall. The face of the woman fingering a lily blooming between indolent legs looked very much like hers.

'The one from Chen's lab?' the girl said.

Her accent suggested southern United States; an expatriate like me, or more probably, given what I'd been able to infer of Jasminder's views, a political refugee. I grunted. The fridge gave a loud rattle when I pulled on the door. I heard an echoing scoff behind me.

'Feel good about what you're doing?' the girl said.

I glanced her way. If I had been less tired, I might have picked up the belligerence in her voice, and got on my own fighting stance. Instead I pulled bacon and tomatoes from my shelf, and wondered if I'd misheard her tone, or if there was any reason why a complete stranger would be rude to me at this hour.

'Feels like research,' I said.

'Because it was not enough when AI companies plundered artists left and right until they could put everybody out of business. Now we need public research to plunder people's brains.'

I thought she glanced at one of the pictures of the wall just then. I remembered that first morning, when I'd heard Jasminder arguing on the phone about payment for her drawings, or rights, or something I'd never been able to ask and had quickly stopped thinking about. *Don't get dragged into political squabbles*, Chen's voice rang in my head. I tossed my dinner into the frying pan and did my best to shrug, though my shoulders were beginning to tense.

'We don't plunder anyone's brain. Half of the university has opted out, and it's all anonymous anyway. We're just trying to know if AI can understand humans. I don't see what's so wrong about that.'

'Aw.' The girl put a hand to her chest, tilting her head to the side. 'Understand humans. Altruistically. How adorable.'

My hand trembled around the handle of the pan. I knew I shouldn't respond. I wouldn't have, if someone else hadn't irrupted into the kitchen just then.

'Could you ventilate the kitchen when you cook meat, Sabrina?' Jasminder snapped, as she threw the window open.

I looked over my shoulder. Jasminder's face was all sweet delight as she bent towards the other woman's face for a kiss. A puff of cool breeze came in. This early in spring, it was unseasonably warm, even for me, and temperatures hadn't been normal when I'd been born. The cold still pricked me unpleasantly, and I fought an urge to fling the window shut again.

'Even if you're unhappy that AI exists, that won't make it less real,' I said. 'We're trying to adjust to it. Understand it. Not just leave it to shady corps. Sneer all you want, but that feels much more productive to me than bitching about what we can't change.'

'Sure. No *shady corps* at all among Chen's private sponsors,' Jasminder said. Her lover guffawed. 'And researching AI is *just* the thing we should be doing right now. Nothing more urgent in the world. No climate breakdown, no – oh, wait.'

She gave the wide-open window a pointed look. I realised that, for all that the draught had felt unpleasant, I wasn't even feeling the need to cover my arms. I took a deep breath, reminding myself that bickering academics were a fact of life.

'This is exactly what we want to tackle,' I said. 'Once AI understands emotion, it will be able to figure out why nothing seems to convince people the climate emergency is real. We're not dealing with rational decision-making. Once we have a program that's powerful enough to understand both the problem and why people resist addressing it –'

'God, she really believes what she's saying, doesn't she?' Jasminder's girlfriend said over me, as if I were a reel on her phone. Then she turned to me with a gaze that was much too cool for a glare. 'Right. That's exactly what they want to do. Tackle climate change, rather than make millions finding even better ways to push content on people once your program can understand what makes them tick.'

'*If* it manages to understand them,' Jasminder cut in. 'If you ask me, that Chen guy has a severe case of Nobelitis.'

Then what are you picking on me for? I thought, and almost said it – before the other girl's interruption saved me from talking and feeling as if I was twelve years old again.

'Yeah, whatever. I'm sure Chen's sponsors are all *that* altruistic. Tar sand barons funding research to make AI understand climate change, because they care. Just like *you* care, right?'

I did in fact; I wanted to say as much, only my jaw felt locked in place, and no words seemed pithy enough to dent that woman's self-assured scorn.

'But hey, congratulations on your smart career moves, Sabrina-girl.'

I should have said something. Or I shouldn't have spoken up in the first place – I no longer knew. I was exhausted; I'd had no one to talk to in person about meaningful things for months, part of me kept hearing Chen's gentle admonitions and felt guilty every time I left the lab before being tired enough to fall asleep on my desk, I couldn't even tell if the project I had crossed the ocean for would ever yield results, I lived with a stranger who despised me and what I did. I stared at them until Jasminder raised an eyebrow with a silent '*What?*' etched on her face, and then I tossed the entire frying pan into the sink, strode out and slammed the door behind me.

ᴨiᴨᴇ

September, year 164 post-disaster

With the torches turned off, the hall is shrouded in a gentle penumbra, all soft curves except where broken glass panels poke through. Draughts chill Rossana's skin when she walks too close to the openings in the walls, and remind her to steer her party inward. As Ishmael had warned, the wall is slanted, and as attractive as the structure might have looked when it was first built, it also means that she can't take its solidity for granted.

Rossana takes out her camera and snaps a few pictures. For her research, of course, but the real joy will be to bring them back home, once she finishes her sabbatical in Tadoussac. The wonder of a world where space was redefined by another species: you can pick up whale song from across the world and hear from relatives on fishing boats halfway across the ocean as if they'd gone to run an errand next door, but aside from a few radio enthusiasts, few people ever bother to ask themselves what is going on in the largely deserted settlements far inland, and picture books only ever tell partial stories, shrouded in exoticism and hearsay. Her son will be delighted to take a look at the inside of the legendary city.

The rope around Rossana's waist gives an abrupt tug and she barely catches herself. When she turns around, Catherine gives an apologetic wince.

'Forgot about the rope,' she says. 'Look at this!'

She lurches forward, tugging on the rope again, and as Rossana and Ishmael stumble behind her, she kneels next to a flat dust-covered piece of furniture, with the telltale dark grey of a screen peeking through. She rubs her hands together, concentrating.

Rossana purses her lips, trying not to let her impatience show as she says, 'Catherine, we don't have much time.'

But Catherine doesn't rise.

'I know. This is *probably* not going to work,' she says. 'But if it does...'

Ishmael watches with a puzzled frown. Then he kneels beside her.

'You think you could get something from *this*?' he says.

She's already begun to pry open the case of the ancient digital display, exposing the circuitry and sorting through the bits and pieces she brought to find what could replace the most damaged parts.

'Sometimes we do,' she says, half-glancing at him with a smile. 'If the hard drives are, say, early post-disaster, they could work almost perfectly. Imagine if bits of the network are still intact and we could access the main servers from here...'

He opens his mouth to answer, but Catherine raises a hand to silence him. Rossana stifles a smile. Then it fades, when she notices a look of genuine embarrassment on his face.

It's a long while before Catherine's focus dissolves into a frown. She shakes her head and begins packing her things in silence. Given how little power must be left in the network, if any, this is the outcome Rossana anticipated. As much as she wishes she could let her niece indulge her hobbies, the attempt is turning into a waste of precious time. She's about to speak, but Ishmael has crouched at Catherine's side again.

'Does it work, sometimes?' he says.

She raises her eyebrows.

'Much of the time, if you have a few hours ahead of you. And a universal screwdriver. And a huge tolerance for frustration.' She pauses. 'Haven't you ever seen pictures?'

He makes a vague gesture.

'I was just wondering. If you could find... Never mind. We need to get going,' he adds with a glance at Rossana.

Indeed they do, but she suddenly feels bad about the way he cut himself short.

'Find what, lost records of something?' she hears Catherine ask gently, after they've fallen in line again.

He grunts something vague and peers at the ground, where a long crack is visible under the leaves. Rossana hesitates. Then she turns to him, and smiles.

'I spent a lot of time looking for whatever information I can find about where my ancestors came from,' she says. 'I've found a few things. Digital archaeology can perform some real feats with old electronics every now and then, I can't deny that.' Catherine gives her a surprised look. She shrugs,. 'The problem is, sometimes we imagine that every second of the past was recorded somewhere, and it can be… very disappointing to realise how little that actually mattered was.'

Who people really loved, what they held on to, what truths they believed, what made them feel under the fragments of personas they relentlessly recorded. She still remembers her dejection upon realising that she would never touch what she had been reaching for. The past was gone. The best that the new world could hope for was to get rid of the bits of poison that kept cropping up here and there, like mines in a forest where battles were lost long ago.

'Anyway. Let's just find the device that AI comes from and disable it, shall we? Ishmael, I assume you've looked at archives? Any idea where old servers might be stored?'

'According to the archives, there shouldn't even be any unaccounted servers in here,' he replies.

He sounds peevish all of a sudden, though whether that's due to Rossana's question or because of the earlier exchange, she couldn't tell. Nobody says anything for a while.

'You know, we don't need to find the server itself,' Catherine says at last. 'If there was a network –'

'Well, that clearly didn't work, did it?' Rossana cuts in.

She turns her attention back to Ishmael, in time to see him and Catherine exchange a glance. He looks at her, and shakes his head, frowning.

'We have no idea why anyone would have hidden a powerful program in here. This was never a facility for computer research. We just – nobody can explain this. Right in the middle of the one place in the city everyone was happy to let crumble in peace. We were hoping you would have ideas,' he adds, as if it was an accusation.

Rossana stares into the empty eyes of another dimetrodon, leaning with its sail thrust at a forty-five degrees angle. Stalks are wound around its legs like layered fetters, longer and stronger than any vine should have been without human intervention.

'I don't have answers, if that's what you mean,' she says. 'Ideas, yes. For one thing, I believe you're right. No one has explored this place since the ivy started growing.'

He raises his eyebrows. 'I *know* I'm right,' he says.

She ignores him. 'This means no one was in a position to turn a computer on in recent years. And it can take decades for AIs to compute every pathway through local firewalls and manage to go rogue. Is there any device that could have kept a computer or server powered in all this time?'

'Not that I know of.'

'Well then.'

She nods to Catherine, who's standing next to her, hefting a hanging branch of ivy and gazing upward with an air of wonder. The young woman starts.

'Remember those articles you found, that we read on the way here?' Rossana prompts.

'Oh.' Catherine drops the branch. 'Well, folks in Tadoussac have been studying this for some time, apparently. Some people attempted to power buildings through photosynthesis, a few years pre-collapse. Never achieved anything much. It's not like there's a lot of energy to divert once the plants have taken their fill. Still... Auntie, do you mean what I think you mean?'

'I'm beginning to have suspicions. But since we're talking about computers, I'll defer to you in this.'

'Oh,' Catherine stammers. She twirls her finger around the tip of the vine, and tugs it towards Ishmael, as if the evidence was self-explanatory. His puzzled attention finally spurs her on.

'When I opened that display, some of the regular power cables did seem to be in bad shape,' she says. 'And we already know some phytoelectric systems are still in place. I wouldn't have thought we'd see one that has managed such a reliable output for so long, but…'

Ishmael looks around.

'You mean…' he says, poking a finger into the ivy.

'That we're looking at the organism that has been keeping your rogue AI alive. Yes.'

And with that, Rossana thinks of harmful strains again, and what may need to happen to this entire building once their mission is over. It pricks at her heart, and she runs her hand through the leaves in a brief caress.

The leaves flutter back, as if a ghost were truly running with the sap, greeting her as she acknowledges it.

Iteration #589DE45A – Still searching

After yesterday's rain, the river churns with mud. And I am jolted with excitement when, in the last rays of the sun, I glimpse your back, pink and silver flashing in the dark flow.

My brother points and shrieks. My heart races as I toss the lure into the water. As usual, it is too rushed, too close, and I prepare for the customary disappointment when my fishing line dangles again freely out of the water. But after mere moments there's a sharp pull, and excitement rises again as I see you dance at the end of the line, and I reel you in, pull you out, grasp your slippery body and hold you as your tail slams left and right in my hand.

I'll be good, I promise; I won't allow it to hurt. I lift a heavy rock and bring it down hard on your head, twice, in quick succession. Your tail stops moving. You're still so bright, so gorgeous. I'm so proud I caught you, and on top of that, so proud I made good on my promise to myself to be humane and not let you suffer.

And then you slam your tail against my hand again.

Dismayed, I hold you still. The blows weren't strong enough. I strike once more, harder, though not hard enough to crush your head – you're so beautiful and I want to keep you that way. Again, you stop twitching. Again, it's only a moment. Excitement has washed away and now I only want it to stop; I can't toss you back into the water – can I? With your head injured, you wouldn't last, and I promised I wouldn't let you suffer – besides, I've wanted to catch one of you for so long, and you're so beautiful, and you're mine. This time I grab you by the tail and slam your entire body against the rocks. Your skin is slippery. It takes more blows, three, maybe four.

I'm so sorry. Don't you understand I had to see this through? You don't let an injured creature back into the water. You put it out of its misery. It's the humane thing to do. I'm sorry it took so long. But it's done now, and you're no longer hurting. Me and my brother, we'll carry you home, everyone will see how beautiful you are, Mum will cook you for dinner and you'll be delicious as only an animal killed in the wild can be, and I can call myself a successful woodsman now that I've caught my first trout.

I'll never go fishing again.

TEN

April, year 1 pre-disaster

I stare at the night out of the window from the tiny desk at my bedside, wondering for the umpteenth time why there were no shutters in this country, why people stayed indoors all the time but still allowed the dawn to wake them up at ungodly hours. I tried to recall the last time I'd let myself enjoy the sunlight, and couldn't remember if it had been on my way back from the fast-food joint or on an afternoon when I'd felt poorly enough to justifying going home before sundown. Windowless labs were their own form of torture.

At least the AI knew about this now, I thought. I had kept feeding it with my brain waves and stream-of-consciousness musings, hundreds of them by now, but lately those had endlessly turned towards memories of the spring – *real* spring, not a season mired in slushy streets and cloudy weather – and bewilderment at how Chen could bear to live this vampiric life, never more than a few steps away from his work.

There came a knock. For one crazy moment, I thought that my mentor had followed me home and was going to ask me to work from my bed. Then Jasminder opened the door.

'Hey,' she said, and held up a large glass lunch box as if it were self-explanatory. It smelled of meat and spices, and my mouth watered in spite of myself. I hadn't had the time to cook anything in a while, either.

'Yes?' was all I could muster the energy to say.

She gave me a tight, awkward smile.

'I went to my mum's this weekend. She basically ordered me to take the leftovers. I don't think she'll ever understand what *vegan* means. She's a great cook, though. Makes a mean butter chicken. No sense is throwing it away, so… you want it?'

I raised an eyebrow.

'You mean, I'm a slightly better destination for your mum's cooking than the rubbish bin? Why, thank you.'

Jasminder bit her lips and scrunched up her nose.

'Okay, that sounded terrible. Sorry.' She took a deep breath. 'Let me try this again? I'm sorry I treated you like shit the other day. That wasn't cool, ganging up on you like that. I don't know why Lana thought it would be okay to pounce on you in the first place. I like that girl, she's great in bed, but God, she's got a mouth…' I raised the other eyebrow. She actually laughed this time. 'That also didn't sound the way I meant it. Let's just say, I'm not sure she understands that not everyone wants to hear her every thought right at the moment when she thinks it. And also, that you don't insult people in their home. I'm sorry about her and I'm sorry I joined in.'

I stared at her in silence. High school mean girl, I'd thought when I'd first met her. Even in slippers and yoga pants, she looked arrogantly cool. Yet she held her box in tense hands, as if nervous at the thought that I might throw her apology back in her face.

'You know, some of us can't afford not to make smart career moves,' I said. 'Not everyone can study humanities and reinvent Marxism on their parents' money. And I meant it when I said I didn't want to leave AI to the wrong people. I don't know if I'm doing this right, but I'm trying.' It would have been a good point at which to stop and so avoid wrecking the moment. But I had spent far too long keeping every thought that wasn't work-related to myself. And they were growing bitter. I didn't stop. 'And for the record, I know about climate breakdown. Maybe you can ignore it when you have an air-conditioned house in Toronto, but where I'm from? You'd have to live in a cave. You can barely stay alive on the Riviera in summer. Ask me when I last took Nonna to the hospital during a heatwave. If you've ever wondered why nobody wants to have children anymore...' I pointed with my thumb at the window behind. 'Does Lana pick fights with every SUV driver out there? Or does she keep her speeches for postdocs who are too broke to afford a car or new clothes?'

Jasminder shrugged, though not angrily.

'When I manage to predict what gets her started, I'll let you know,' she says. 'Oh, and I work in bioengineering, not humanities. But fair point.'

I raised an eyebrow. I had been convinced that Jasminder was an art student; she certainly seemed to spend more time with a sketchpad in hand than a laptop.

'What, surprised?' she said.

Then, just as I was trying to come up with an answer that would not embarrass me, I remembered her phone conversation. Then the real upset in her girlfriend's voice when she'd mentioned AI robbing artists of their jobs. Some tiny part of the picture I had failed to grasp until now came into clearer focus.

'You're a professional artist,' I said. 'And you're not finding work because everybody uses AI? Is that right?'

She looked at me with surprise, or maybe something more complex.

'It's getting almost impossible, yes. Nobody wants to pay what art is really worth when they can click on a button for free and get something people will be just as satisfied with.' She waved a hand. 'No big deal. I never really believed I'd break through.'

It occurred to me that I would have needed much more money in my family to even attempt to make a living at something as fickle as art. I also knew, just as certainly, that to Jasminder this *was* a big deal. And that no matter what I thought about it, it stood to reason that her girlfriend would be upset on her behalf, too.

'I'm sorry,' I said.

She shook her head.

'Don't worry about it. As I said, this was doomed from the start.'

'And so you fell back on bioengineering.' I considered this for a moment, then attempted a smile. 'Another field that's entirely concerned with the good of humankind, right?'

She scrunched her nose again, then grinned.

'Shut up,' she said. Then she thrust the box forward. 'You want this or not?'

I stood up.

'I've got some leftover General Tso tofu I was going to throw away,' I said. 'Want to share?'

She grinned again and hopped towards the kitchen.

ELEVEN

September, year 164 post-disaster

'This? The ivy? How on Earth would those plants get energy to the machine?' Ishmael says, as they move towards the ruined door.

Catherine takes two hopping steps over a fragile-looking hollow, and answers without looking at Rossana first, this time.

'Here's the thing. No one knows for sure,' the young woman says. 'It's not like you can plug a cord into a plant. Somehow, some folks managed to adapt the designs of wireless chargers to make them pick up on whatever energy plants could spare. They must have thought that building devices that would charge themselves as soon as their owners walked through a park would be a good solution when the grids started breaking down. To the best of my knowledge, though, you'd need a jungle, not a park. Or…' she trailed off, gesturing at the greenery around them.

Ishmael frowns, as if torn between awe for an astonishing feat of technology and the displeasure that hasn't left him since they entered the building. Catherine's smile is almost apologetic.

'Though I'd say this entire place could perhaps power a single server, but no more,' she says. 'Else I would have managed to get something from the digital displays. It's a miracle that even part of it has kept running all this time. The slightest drop in output would likely be enough for the power to become insufficient.'

'You mean, we could burn away some of the ivy and solve our problem?' Ishmael replies.

Rossana pauses, briefly, staring up. It strikes her anew, every time, how beautiful these places are. Like caves, like works of art, like the edge of human understanding, beckoning and forbidding at the same time.

Like tragic endings.

She turns to Ishmael.

'I'll need to take samples once this is over. There's a chance that we will have to destroy it all, yes.'

He starts.

'Why on Earth…?'

'Any strain that could invade virgin ecosystems needs to be removed. You said this one hasn't been studied. I don't know for certain yet, but seeing how vigorous it looks… Do you know what could happen if seeds landed in a forest?'

'I suppose,' he says. He still has a bewildered frown. 'But you'd have to destroy the entire street. People graze their goats on the ivy nearby, they have birds roosting there –'

'I know. And I'm sorry. I'll advise against it if that's an option at all. We just can't risk another Florida.'

They've reached the door. The floor is brittle here; they have been balancing their last steps on the toughest branches they could find, and peering at times through holes in the masonry. Rossana darts her torch and the beam returns a glint from a glass case, jewels that no one thought of looting, busy as the world was wrangling pandemics and watching the human population dwindle to insignificance while forests and whales breathed a sigh of relief.

Behind her, Ishmael raises his voice, saying, 'You can't just suggest that people blow the whole street up and go build their fields elsewhere after all the trouble we've...'

There's another resin model right behind the glass case, a hint of something tawny, like fur between leaves. She pauses. Usually museums kept geology exhibits separate from the ones on biology, but...

The ground crumbles under her next step.

The torch clatters to the ground. Catherine yelps and tries to grab her, to no avail. Debris of dead wood hurtle down as her leg goes through, and just as she notices the rotten patch hidden under a trailing branch, her other knee hits the ground, breaking through rotting wood and concrete alike; then her entire body goes through, is jolted to halt initially as the rope between herself and her companions pulls taut, then again, which she presumes must be her weight dragging Catherine to her knees.

A moment later, she's found her bearings. Her eyes adjust to the penumbra again, and she pulls herself against the rope.

'Nothing hurts,' she calls. 'Can you pull me up?'

'Yeah, just – oh shit. Auntie – *Oh fuck!*'

The rope jolts Rossana again, and there's a sound of crashing debris down below, and then it's Ishmael's turn to shriek, and then there's another sound, not human at all.

And then she understands. That thing she took for a resin model. She shouts Catherine's name.

'Catherine, don't run!' she calls, quite uselessly, seeing as the safety line between them holds both Catherine and Ishmael tethered in place.

Her hands instinctively reach for the rope, to hoist herself back up through the hole, but she stops herself at the last moment. She's heard the growl again, and remembers the lynx – though this isn't the sound a lynx makes. There are mountain lions in this country, and they're large enough to assume that a prone human could be prey. And Catherine –

Catherine must still be down, unable to stand with Rossana's body dangling at the end of the rope pinning her in place. Fear grips Rossana, so firmly that she has to choke back the sound that wants to escape her mouth. She cannot make a move. She needs to be still enough to minimise her own weight and allow Catherine to stand up again. She reaches up, tries to hoist herself, fails. Her mouth goes dry.

'Don't turn your backs,' she calls again, unable to keep the panic out of her voice. 'Stand firm. Hold your jackets open. Make yourselves bigger. Show it you can defend yourselves!'

She doesn't know if a mountain lion will be as easy to scare off as a lynx. Catherine is trapped by the safety line. If the beast recognises that she is defenceless, there is nothing she can do against an attack. Rossana stretches her arm, almost finds purchase, then her hand slips. She cries out.

Then there's a metallic sound, and, belatedly, she remembers that North Americans still carry guns – and the fear overwhelms her.

'For the love of God, don't shoot!' she screams before she can help herself.

'Okay.' Catherine's voice again, calmer now. 'Okay. You heard the lady. We're not going to shoot you. Good kitty. Back off now. Kitty kitty kitty. Please.'

'Lady needs to explain why we can't shoot,' Ishmael says.

There's a metallic click.

'Ishmael, don't! You'll –'

'Oh *shit! GET AWAY FROM US! FUCK!*'

And with that there's the report of the gun, once, twice, and Rossana closes her eyes.

The growling has stopped. Or she thinks it has. Her ears are ringing. She's never heard a gun fire before. Her whole body freezes. She should have known. The old ways are still alive inland, even the ones that led to the collapse. Animals die just for being in the way. She barely realises that Catherine and Ishmael have begun to pull her out. As soon as her feet are back on solid branches, she flings her arms around her niece.

'Are you all right? Did it come close?'

Catherine shakes her head. Her face has gone an awful shade of pale, however.

Rossana looks at Ishmael, at the gun she now notices, poking under the edge of his jacket. She could thank him. She will have to, when she's recovered from the shock. A *gun.* This man was carrying something that could doom them all, and he didn't bother to tell her. And he saved her niece.

She lets go of Catherine, and looks around for the cat's corpse.

'Where is it?' she says at last.

Ishmael points at a hole between ivy trunks. She sets out in that direction. He grabs her arm.

'What on Earth are you doing?'

'If it's wounded, we need to –'

'Wounded?'

His eyes widen.

'I just shot above its head to scare it off. I'm not a monster. Clearly it didn't think our jackets were too frightening,' Ishmael says.

She opens her mouth. Closes it. There's an uncomfortable silence.

'Well,' Rossana says at last. 'That's one disaster averted.'

And only then – because as little as she knows Ishmael, she is relieved that he retained a cool head, and that they did not end up killing a crucial apex predator in the heat of the moment – she trains her eyes on the other thing she had been worrying about.

Overhead, where the bullet must have buried itself in the concrete wall, there's a streak of light green over the darker leaves. So this is one of *those* strains then. It is too slow to see just yet, but the shift in colour is tell-tale: buds stirring under bark, ready to sprout new growth where they felt the damage hit, in less time than it will take them to safely exit the building again.

'We're going to need those machetes after all if we don't get moving right now,' she sighs.

Iteration #5F6593A1 – Still searching

I am wary, but I make myself look happy for you. After much insistence on your part, I've ordered a salad, and I am now poking around my plate, waiting for a dry leaf to disintegrate in my mouth and savouring the watery flavour. I'm hungry, unbelievably so. There is hunger coursing in my veins and tingling my fingertips, or maybe it is just the way my blood pressure drops every time I shift in my chair. I poke around, eating nothing. I feel much too strong to yield, and that, in itself, is so intoxicating that mere satiety will never match it.

You ask questions with a casual air that is so transparently fake I could laugh. Of course I feel fine, I say. No, I don't think I've been losing weight, does it look as if I have? It must be my clothes. But thank you, all the same. I wish I could tell you the truth and let you know how proud I am that you could now circle my waist with both hands, that there isn't a gram of fat, soft, repulsive tissue left anywhere I can touch. But you wouldn't understand. You don't know how good it is to feel invincible, to have mastered yourself so thoroughly you can command your own hunger.

No, I'm not really hungry, let's go. Great restaurant, though. We should come back one of these days. Yes, I feel perfectly fine, why do you ask?

What could a psychiatrist even do for me? Help yourself to what's left, really. It's delicious. Everything is delicious. Too much sunlight and the noise like the ocean in my ears and the hunger that feels like a pitiful mewling inside that I never have to listen to again and how I feel like I could soar high enough to touch the stars –

My legs buckle under me. I hear your voice in a brief cry, and all I feel is surprise.

TWELVE

May, year 1 pre-disaster

'There *is* one good thing about American coffee,' I said.

Zeyneb, the biologist I'd met on my first day and who still shared the workspace with me from time to time, raised her eyebrows as far as the ceiling. I matched her expression.

'You can drink it at six in the afternoon and still sleep like a baby afterward. And it almost tastes like coffee.'

Zeyneb scoffed, but she was still smiling.

'You can have my mug as a souvenir, then,' she said, getting up and stretching.

'Are you going anywhere?'

'Home.'

That took me aback. I'd enjoyed Zeyneb's sporadic presence, though too much work had prevented the pleasantness from growing into real friendship. It had not occurred to me to ask when her contract would end, or what she would do then.

I didn't even know where her home was, come to think of it, and felt too silly to ask. I had a brief thought of my own sun-drenched town, half a world away.

'That's wonderful!' I said, because I didn't know what else would do. 'Are you... still going to work with chimps?'

'Maybe. Or not. Whoever gives me money, I suppose.' 'I'm not so big on chimps, to be honest. If I can find someone to pay me to study whale communication again, I'll be a happy woman. As for right now, let's call it a holiday? Unpaid, and with my last paper to finish? Woo-hoo!'

She seemed less disgruntled than her words suggested, however. She began stacking things in a neat pile in front of her screen. She made an 'Ah-ha!' sound when she reached the mug hidden behind the papers in her drawer, the one with the picture of a pod of orcas, and set it down in front of me.

Looking at the sinuous creatures, blissfully alone in their sea of blue porcelain, I had a sudden thought of dolphins swimming in the deserted canals of Venice, in the stories my mother used to tell me of the time of my birth. And then another, on the cusp of my teens: walking along an equally deserted beach in Sanremo and watching dolphins swim closer, undeterred for once by sailing ships and cruise boats, during a new pandemic that buffeted an already tired world, my already poor family.

Home.

Zeyneb was still tidying, her back to me.

'I'm glad to go home, anyway. Go to the beach. Gorge on some real food. Try to talk my grandfather out of doing the Hajj this year. Holiday stuff.'

'What's wrong with the Hajj?' I said.

'Hot cycle, that's what's wrong.' I must have looked blank. She shook her head, indulgent. 'Hajj season will fall right in the middle of summer for a few more years. And every year, people die of heat by the thousands. Out of a couple of million it's not that huge, but…'

She trailed off and waved her hand as if it didn't matter much, and then she pushed the pile of papers and pencils into a bag, and I felt my throat tighten. I rose.

'My Nonna has been having a hard time every summer for years,' I said. 'Keep the old man safe, will you?'

She looked up, surprised, and the next second was very still and awkward – then we hugged, as if we hadn't missed almost a year's opportunity to become something more than strangers.

Later, I pushed my bike through dwindling traffic, watched the fragmented reflection of the sun disappear from the skyscrapers like setting stars, and as I hoped that Zeyneb would soon get to stand on a beach and converse with a whale, I wondered what I was going to hope for myself.

Jasminder was already home, lounging on the sofa and doodling on a sketch pad. She was alone, which I was grateful for; Lana had been showing up around the flat, but had hardly thawed, though she no longer confronted me. I much preferred evenings when there was no one home but Jasminder and I.

The détente had taken an unexpected turn. After her apologies, we had stood in embarrassed silence by the microwave, as the butter chicken warmed. The smell had been wonderful. I'd said so, after a while, to break the awkwardness. And we had started talking.

And we hadn't stopped, not until we were halfway through the night and both exhausted enough that we could have fallen asleep standing up. I'd talked about Italy, growing to adulthood in a country that had embraced fascism in all but name, one of a handful of children people still bothered to have. She'd talked about childhood in Canada, in a family of academics that felt increasingly isolated in their progressive ways as casual authoritarianism seeped up from the United States; the high school girlfriend who'd introduced her to drawing and the Indigenous friends who'd got her into environmental activism; the thousand hilarious things that had happened to her along the way. Laughter had caught me by surprise, just as I was telling myself that it would take more than silly anecdotes to stop me being angry at her. She was very smart, I had to admit, and she knew how to tell a story. And she cared about other people much more than she seemed to, in her own prickly, awkward way. And she and I saw eye to eye on a great many things I had not imagined – had not *wanted* to imagine – before.

The day after that, we'd begun talking about Italian heatwaves, Canadian fires, pandemics and the many disasters we'd already lived through, and how we'd both sensed as soon as we could talk that we were growing up at the end of the world; and we'd stayed up late again. And it happened again the following day. And all of a sudden, my entire life had seemed much brighter.

Jasminder waved.

'I hope you're hungry,' she said.

I wasn't – I rarely was any longer – but I could eat something, which has become a more or less permanent state, fed by coffee and hasty snacks. I said so. Jasminder shot up. Moments later, I heard the microwave and smelled something richly fragrant in the kitchen.

'Brought some of my mum's saag paneer,' she said, and added when I looked nonplussed – 'Cheese and mustard greens. Go on. It's delicious.'

'Is it vegan?' I said, raising an eyebrow.

'Of course not. I told you my mum doesn't understand vegan. And she'll be even more confused now that I've asked her for the leftovers. Oh well.'

'Why did you do that?' I said.

'For you, silly. Go on, eat.'

I did. The spices burned my mouth in a wonderfully satisfying way. I'd spent the last months swearing to my mother on the phone that I ate correctly, but the truth was, I rarely bothered to cook any more. Sitting down at the kitchen table felt like a lovely, restful luxury.

Jasminder rubbed my shoulders when I told her. She liked touching, and being touched – another thing I hadn't known about her. Her touch felt like a kitten roughhousing my foot: enthusiastic, too blunt, unexpectedly endearing.

'Eating crap won't make your research better. It will just make you a masochist. And if you're really into that, I have a ex-girlfriend I can recommend instead.' She wagged her eyebrows. 'So eat.'

She watched me as I did. It felt good to feel full, and even better to have indulged in the time it took to enjoy the food.

She was right, too. If failing to take proper meals was the way to improve my research, I clearly needed to punish myself a lot more.

I sighed. 'Sometimes this whole thing feels like I'm lost in the jungle looking for Eldorado,' I said. 'With Chen swearing we're getting closer and we're too good to use a compass.'

'That would be a cool story to write,' Jasminder said, smiling.

'Don't get me started on writing. I've done enough for a lifetime. God.'

'For research?' she said, her voice quiet, attentive.

I paused. Jasminder and I had not talked about my research again, an unspoken agreement that our new friendship didn't need to be chafed at for the sake of scoring points. I hadn't expected her question to touch me so directly. She mistook my hesitation for diffidence.

'Change the subject?' she said.

'No!' I forced a carefree expression. 'It's fine. Even Chen doesn't know all I'm doing anyway. It's driving me slowly crazy, that's all.'

She nodded, listening.

'You already know what he's after,' I said. 'He thinks we can teach AI to understand human emotions, the way he managed to predict chimp behaviour. He's been collecting recordings of brain waves and tagging them with standardised words, and then trying to see if the AI could make its own predictions.' I paused. 'It can't. Whatever he says.'

'So you spend your time tagging random brainwaves?' Jasminder said.

'That's the gist of it. Only, I've been trying something new.' I tried to summon an enthusiasm I no longer felt, and gave up. 'I don't think tagging works. I just don't believe emotions are that simple. Say, oh I don't know – that feeling when you thought your roommate sucked, and then she started bringing you food and being the absolute coolest person, and you feel stupid but also know you'd probably be bingeing on antidepressants if she wasn't around – how the hell do you tag *that*?'

She gaped at me, then burst out laughing.

'Fair enough,' she said. 'So, your solution...?'

'I make recordings of my own brainwaves. I try describing exactly what I'm feeling at that exact moment. And then I go have a cup of coffee, and then I go again. I try to look at pictures, read the news, remember things. Anything that can make me feel as many things as I can. And I let the AI learn.'

Jasminder whistled.

'Problem is, I'm just one person. I can spend as many hours as I like doing this, I'll never produce the kind of volume an AI needs. I have millions of samples without tags, a few thousands with Chen's stupid one-word tags, and a few hundred of mine. It would take a miracle.'

'But you keep going.'

'Well. Nobody knows how AIs work, really. I might as well, right? Though, if you ask me, I'm going to spend the rest of forever in the jungle.'

Jasminder grunted and nodded, but didn't add anything. After a while, she patted my arm.

'You're making a living. And you're not hurting anyone. You can take that and stop worrying, no?'

I thought of Zeyneb and her resigned satisfaction with her job. It felt a bit depressing, but pragmatic; and pragmatic was as much as I could aspire to, if I was honest.

Unless this was just another excuse for being selfish, focusing the energy of an entire life of a pursuit that helped nothing and no-one but me and my career. I would not have expected Jasminder to champion that sort of mindset; then again, she was probably just being kind.

The world was turning into a very small place. One where I could decide that the only human that mattered was me – and the looming presence of Professor Chen, the god that presided over my existence and future.

And my roommate. I still had that, at least.

'Your mother truly is a fabulous cook,' I said, and I meant it.

Then, as on most nights, I got ready to keel over from exhaustion.

Thirteen

September, year 164 post-disaster

They're halfway up the stairs when the new buds begin to unfold. At Rossana's instructions, Ishmael is weaving a couple of supple branches across a gap in the steps, so that they'll have something to catch them if the growth along the walls cannot support their weight while they climb. He swears and pulls his hand away when a tendril of ivy wraps itself around his finger.

'Sorry,' he says when Catherine starts.

Rossana puts a hand on his shoulder. She's still wrestling with how much the incident earlier shook her. She *has* been terrified for Catherine, and in disbelief of her own choice to let her come to Toronto in spite of her lack of experience, in spite of how dangerous rewilded buildings sometimes turn out to be. And then there was the gun. She has no words for that one. The stunned terror following the report, the stomach-gripping fear that she and her niece had just entrusted their safety to someone who might *kill on sight*.

She might as well be honest. She's disliked Ishmael from the start.

She's beginning to suspect that she's been unfair to him, regardless. He's obviously been on edge ever since they started. Bio-architectural structures sometimes have that effect on people, a bone-deep fear that the disquieting atmosphere inherent to ruined and abandoned places could not explain alone. Formerly dead places growing into life forms of their own, where humans are not welcome. She cannot really blame him.

'Don't worry,' she says, and it surprises her how naturally the words come. 'It will grow fast for awhile, but not fast enough to trap us if we keep moving. We won't be able to set up camp in here now, though, and we definitely won't be able to leave and come back later.' Not unless they destroy the ivy first, but even if it turns out to be necessary, there would be no way to eradicate the entire plant before the AI spread itself irreversibly though every communication device in the city, not if they want to do it carefully enough to preserve the fields and houses in the area. 'We'll have to stay on the move until we find what we're looking for.'

Ishmael runs a finger along the new green sprout, as if making a tentative offer of peace.

'Did I really do that? With my gun?'

Rossana doesn't answer straight away. Come to think of it, she is a little embarrassed of how much the gunshot scared her. She catches Catherine's hand to help her jump over two crumbled steps.

'Some strains were engineered to react to mechanical shock, yes,' she says. 'A last-ditch attempt to prevent deteriorated buildings from collapsing on people, I believe. I'm not sure how they managed that. I apologise for not warning you. People don't carry guns in Italy, so I didn't think of checking.'

He looks at her as if he had not expected her to apologise.

'I didn't think I would need it either,' he says.

Then he gets up. They exchange a wary glance.

'I suppose you're going to recommend destruction, aren't you?' he says, his voice neutral.

Rossana catches herself just before she starts telling him about proper protocol, analyses and collective decisions. Instead she reaches out to a light green tip, already curling up in search for a place where it could attach itself. A strange, abnormal, gigantic baby, orphaned and grasping for survival.

That cougar had been grasping for survival too. None of them would have considered killing it for that. She attempts a smile.

'That would be the prescribed step,' she says. 'which doesn't mean we shouldn't think it through.'

She gently pulls her foot free of a coiled stalk. Broken petioles cut in shiny green. She imagines the creature registering the pain and reacting with a minute chemical wail.

'Just tell me one thing, though, Rossana,' Ishmael says. 'Are you truly feeling all right in this place?'

She doesn't speak at once. She thinks of the dimetrodon downstairs, beasts dead for so many million years that the distance is incomprehensible. Post-collapse, humans might deserve a place by their side, a once-thriving species that a slew of diseases, wars and climatic disasters reduced to less than a tenth of its former might, before the regrowth of cities and the alliance with the whales opened up new, fragile paths for the survivors to tread for a little while longer. But her discomfort is not philosophical in nature. Every time she pauses, opens her senses to figure out the best way ahead, something whispers in her mind, a presence, or a myriad of them, like a shadow at the corner of her eye.

'I don't, no,' she admits.

His look is gentler when he turns to her again. 'Then let's go find this thing and get out of here.'

'We'd better,' Catherine says. 'What with all that new growth, we've just given it enough fuel for a century or two.'

Rossana nods and they exchange a glance. This was the last conversation they had during their evening on the ship, right before Catherine curled up on the bunk and waved her good night then fell asleep while Rossana was still halfway through a sentence. Should they find a server to destroy, they'd better hope that it is the only place where the rogue AI's main program is stored. She'd once made five different forays into the same building – a former bank – in search for every last backup of a particularly resilient malware. That bank had been nowhere as far gone as the museum, and the malware there had been pre-emptively destroyed before it had begun to show up in comms. But the attempt they're making now will be the only one they have, and she wonders if their chance of success has come and gone already. Though they've just spent the better part of the day combing the place for doors hidden behind the green, they could already have missed many, and she doesn't want to think of how much harder the task will be, now that the sun is beginning to go down and the gunshot has spurred the ivy into a frenzy of growth. Meanwhile, comms outside are down, and whales may have sent word of the next coming storm, for all they know.

But then she thinks of something else, and smiles.

'Now we know that there are predators here, we'll need to be noisier,' she says. 'I'll take the first turn singing.'

She twines her fingers into the ivy on the wall, caressing a smooth leave with her thumb. 'Apologies, my pretty one,' she whispers. 'Don't tell me you've also evolved to grow when you're sung to, will you?'

And she starts crawling along, launching into a Fairuz song which her mother used to sing her to sleep with.

Iteration #6AC547F5 – Still searching

Stuck in traffic, the city droning all around, your voice saying something I distantly hear, a thousand little things I should be thinking of before my departure – though none of them as vivid right now as your kiss that lingers on my lips, and the anticipation and dread of the parting kiss to come – and then I feel your hand on my knee, gently travelling up, and I forget everything, even to breathe.

You're speaking again, and I think I answer, though how the words leave my throat I have no idea. We crawl through the streets as if through honey, and your hand lingers on my thigh, centimetres away from where I desperately need it, trapped under mine, and I hold your fingers as if I could ever hold them tight enough to make your warmth stay with me forever, as maddening as it feels, and there's a thousand things I want to say but none will leave my mouth and I can only hope you'll hear them all the same, you'll understand even though there are no words to tell you how much I want time to stop.

But it won't, I know – and very soon there will be goodbye, and the gates of the airport, and then days and weeks and months of missing you.

Fourteen

August, day 0

I stared at the screen like a fool, coffee cooling in my hand, reading the words over and over and wondering what mistakes could have caused them to appear there.

I had not written this. My love life had been far too uneventful for feelings of that intensity. The sample bore a number I knew was not one of mine. Either this had been a quirk of chance, a billion digital monkeys typing random letters and chancing upon actual meaning, or...

I entered a new sample. Sentences came up on the screen, and I read them, truly read them, as they kept making sense in front of my eyes. There was a third sample, then a fourth, all equally coherent. My breath quickened and my fingertips prickled. I had done it. It had worked.

I'd written none of those sentences, yet I might have. I had trained the program to write like I did; to *think* like I did. No one in the lab had managed such a thing. The machine had never been able to make sense of the brain waves it was fed, or if it did, had never been able to express in a way a human could understand. And now it did, without a word from me, with no other prompting than the samples I'd loaded. This was unprecedented. It was...

A complete failure.

I'd thought I was helping. Instead I'd biased Chen's brainchild beyond recognition. How had I assumed that I could be lucid enough about my own feelings that I could pretend my musings would reflect the reality of all of humankind?

I made coffee, paced about the room, sat down again. Checked my email, out of compulsion. Chen requested my presence in his office to discuss the publication of our next paper. A charity alerted me to the direness of the situation in Mecca.

I had no idea what was going on in Mecca. The next thing I knew was that the pointer was over the header, and I was clicking.

And reading.

It was as if the words a human being had written did not make half as much sense, at first, as the output of Chen's AI. I read the same sentences over and over, my mouth hanging open, my hands beginning to shake in horror. *Heatwave* and *wet bulb* and *unprecedented* and *stampede* and *seventy thousand dead*. I read that one again. Not thousands, surely. Seventy people would have been bad enough, heatwaves could not...

The word *thousands* blinked in front of my eyes. I kept reading. Then I searched, frantically, for one article after another, but only found confirmation that I was not dreaming.

The heatwave had struck Mecca while I was asleep. As they had very briefly before, temperatures soared to lethal levels. Except this time they had stayed there. Those pilgrims who could afford the luxury hotels around the site had locked themselves in with their air conditioning. Security guards had begun to shoot into the increasingly panicked crowds that attempted to get in. And the heat had kept climbing.

Seventy thousand people had succumbed in the scorching sun, with the tally still rising, while I grumpily woke up and dragged my feet to work as if work was the worst life could offer me.

I remembered Zeyneb's grandfather. I hadn't even tried to get in touch with her since she'd gone.

I didn't notice when Chen entered the lab. I switched tabs, in a daze, and showed him my results. He clapped his hands and patted me on the shoulder, saying things that resembled congratulations and talking about breakthroughs and how we had cracked the future of artificial intelligence.

'Wait,' I said at last. 'I'm sorry I didn't tell you. I trained it myself. I'm the one who fed it emotions, it's just replicating –'

'What an excellent thought! This invalidates nothing, Sabrina. Your brain is as human as anyone else's. Your brainwaves taught it what it needed.'

I poked my finger at the screen in helpless frustration.

'Look at this one. *Look*. Do you really think brain waves can spell "trout"?' My voice was rising. 'And even if you're going to tell me that evolution wired us to look for fish, here's another! Can brain waves spell "book"? Really?'

I caught my head in my hands. Over seventy thousand dead. And I was arguing with my mentor over whether a machine could read minds. Chen touched my shoulder and brought his face down to my level.

'This is even better than anything we'd anticipated. You've just managed to read the collective subconscious, Sabrina. The mind that governs all minds. The reason we can understand one another at all. Can you imagine what we can do with this?'

I stared at him, aghast. A bad case of Nobelitis, Jasminder had said. *Seventy thousand dead, because the luxury hotels wouldn't let them into air-conditioned lobbies.*

Did he even *know* about Zeyneb's grandfather?

Chen smiled and patted my arm.

'You look exhausted. Take the rest of the day off. You've earned it. I'll review the journals we could send this too. This is probably too early for *Nature*, but the biggest consumer studies journals will be thrilled, without a doubt. We'll discuss it tomorrow.'

I mumbled something that could have passed for gratitude, and stomped out.

I cycled through red lights and tears, bumping over endless stretches of construction work until I got home, my face soggy, my head aching. I fumbled with the lock, threw my handbag to the ground, sat down on the doormat and swore between sobs while slamming my hand against the door.

It opened. Jasminder froze upon seeing me, then bend down to help me up.

'Sabrina! What –?'

'Don't you dare ask me what's fucking wrong! Not you, too!' I threw my handbag across the room. I couldn't understand. I'd never understood anything. 'There's seventy thousand people dead because the Earth is boiling up, and I'm sitting in an office and feeding my own brain to AI and flying across the world to conferences that help no one and nothing except my career, and I pretend I'm doing something useful! And Chen went on about collective consciousness as if that wasn't utterly fucking crazy, and he says we're going to save the world eventually, except it's a little too early for that and so for now we're just going to send the result to consumer studies folks! Because they're all about saving the world! And I've been acting as if it was normal, and… fuck this, Jasminder. I know I'm preaching to the choir. I just need to say it.'

But Jasminder only opened her arms and pulled me against her.

'Go ahead and preach. It's so beautiful when people change their minds,' she said.

My jaw went slack. The surprise was so strong that it took me seconds to realise how wonderful it felt to be hugged. I wiped my nose and rested my head on her shoulder. I no longer wanted to cry.

After a while, I slumped on the sofa. Jasminder sat next to me, facing me, her tilted head resting on her folded arm and her bangs draping messily across her forehead. She listened while I spoke, not very coherently. After having broken down on our doorstep and left a trace of snot on her sleeve, I didn't feel much concerned about coherence. I felt empty, and terribly sad, and nothing had meaning anymore. I eventually trailed off with a sigh.

'What are you going to do now?' Jasminder said.

I threw both arms in the air.

'Something stupid. I have no freaking idea. Maybe I'm going to get abjectly drunk. Or go out and get a full-body tattoo. Or I'll start propositioning you, who knows.' She raised an eyebrow while her mouth did an uncertain quirk. I waved my hands. 'Okay, not propositioning you. Fine.'

'No offence,' she said, gently.

'None taken.' I smiled. It felt a little forced, but only a little. 'I've never had sex with a woman anyway. I'd probably suck at it.'

The stare she gave me was full of barely contained mirth.

'Did you really just say that?' she said.

I opened my mouth. Thought, this time. I felt myself go red in the face as she burst out laughing, and I followed suit.

'Sounds like I don't even need to get drunk,' I said.

Jasminder rose.

'*Need* is overrated. I've got a killer bottle of wine. Come on.'

FiFtEEn

September, year 164 post-disaster

By the time they clear the stairs, the new growth is already thick enough to impede their progress. Rossana picks up a faint sound of crumbling masonry. She recalls an old man once, telling her that bioengineered ivy had been no better than a deal with the devil, sacrificing cities by giving them a semblance of immortal life. She found the phrasing so incongruous then that she laughed. She doesn't know why it's stayed with her. Perhaps because she likes the idea that the devil can be kind to plants, if nothing else.

She shakes a curtain of ivy, less gently than she had before. A cloud of bats flies off; she ducks just in time. It is when the sleeve of a jacket drapes around her arm that she starts. The fabric is mostly decomposed, tangled among the leaves, but the stronger threads, embroidered with beads, still hold. Her heart skips a beat, as she thinks she's stumbled upon a lost body. When she realises that this is just another exhibit, she expects to feel better – but doesn't. She pulls the jacket out and folds it on the ground. It feels like laying a ghost to rest.

They stop soon after. Ishmael pulls squares of dark lentil cake out of his backpack and they munch in silence.

Rossana slumps, her leg hanging over the edge of a hole in the floor. She can't even feel the masonry; her knees rest against a branch that has just sprouted a lush web of tendrils, and she shifts every now and then to prevent them from attaching themselves to her trousers. Every part of her is tired: muscles, mind and nerves. Her senses have been on alert for several hours now, and she hasn't even managed to avoid the very dangers she was looking out for, crumbly floors and dangerous tenants. They're no nearer to finding clues, only combing through the building, slower and more painstakingly than before, with the light from the setting sun now almost useless.

Catherine squirms against the ivy, vainly trying to find a comfortable spot. Her face is drawn. She stares at the food in her hand for a long time before biting off a corner, with no visible pleasure or even relief. She suppresses a shiver; the air has grown much cooler since the ivy began its new growth spurt, sucking energy from what little sunlight was coming in and from the very air around them. Rossana squeezes her knee in silence. She keeps picturing her niece trying to get off the ground, facing a predator that would not have been shy about attacking prone, trapped prey, and all because Rossana stepped in the wrong place, after spending so long lecturing them about caution. She can't bear to imagine where they would be now, if Ishmael had not scared the cougar off. She swallows, and does her best not to appear unsettled. They still both look to her as their guide, even though she wonders if she truly deserves that trust.

Ishmael suddenly starts and jumps to his feet.

'Did you hear that?'

Rossana lifts a hand. She's heard nothing; or *heard* is not exactly the word. There's still a sensation she cannot place, and she's counting how many hours they have left until the need to sleep forces them out – at the rate the ivy is growing, they cannot sleep in here without risk of being smothered in a tangle of new leaves, and they cannot spend the night outside without jeopardising the very possibility of exploring the place at all. Ishmael's gunshot may only be partly to blame. This is the building's way of reminding them that it will not extend its welcome forever.

'We find this server, we disable it, we go,' she says, to herself, her companions or the place around them, she doesn't know.

Something touches her hand where it rests against the ground, like a cat looking for attention. She doesn't move yet. On an odd impulse, she thinks very hard, as if she could be heard that way, *I'm sorry. I don't want to destroy you, but we just have to preserve the rest of the world, don't you see? Please let us find what we want and we'll go.*

Her skin feels the faint squeeze of a curling tendril. She withdraws it.

Catherine stands up abruptly.

'Over there!'

She tugs at her line, motioning Rossana and Ishmael to follow, and through hanging vines and blooming branches, makes her excruciatingly slow way towards a flat surface, under a layer of dust.

She pokes at it.

'Digital display. I knew it!'

Rossana sighs.

'You've already tried this. Let's get moving before –'

She gasps in shock as the rope pulls her sharply downwards and stops her mid-step.

Catherine tuts and tugs on the rope once more. Bewildered, Rossana drops to an awkward crouch. Catherine kneels, facing her, in front of the display, still holding the rope in one hand; she grabs her shoulder with the other.

'I *know* you don't believe this will work,' Catherine says, waving the rope for emphasis. 'Not your methods, not your thing, I understand. But we don't need to have that hard drive in hand to get something from it. It's been done before. I can do this now.'

'We've already wasted time once, downstairs. And that was back when we still had time!'

Catherine grabs her shoulders.

'I couldn't make it work downstairs because that happened *before Ishmael fired that round*,' she says. 'Remember? How the ivy is feeding electricity into the entire system? And how we've just given it more power than it's had in decades?'

'How can you even know you've accessed the right server?'

'*Because I'm a digital archaeologist!* Finding useful stuff in a corroded mess – this is what I've done for years!'

She doesn't wait for an answer. She spreads her backpack open on the floor and arranges screwdrivers by size. She hands a small crank to Ishmael.

'I'm going to need to power my equipment. Do you mind? Auntie, if you can just keep an eye on my things so that the plants don't run away with my tools, that would be splendid.'

Rossana stares at her. Ishmael stares at her.

Then they both come forward to do as Catherine's told them.

Ishmael begins to turn the crank, keeping an even speed. In moments, Catherine has set up a small computer and arranged wires; she starts working at the display, splitting the case open and connecting her implements to its open innards. She beams at Ishmael, once, when lights flicker on her own screen.

'Welcome to the mad world of digital archaeology,' she says, and grins. 'I'm going to need a little more kick.'

The whirr intensifies as Ishmael turns faster. After a little while, the lights on the screen grow steady. Catherine works in silence, occasionally clicking her tongue in frustration. Rossana keeps the ivy away from the tiny tools, careful to avoid breaking branches and triggering a new growth spur. She turns around from time to time, to spy for large animals. Ishmael passes around some more lentil cake with one hand. Catherine keeps working, typing away, sometimes tweaking live components and causing flashes of light to course over her screen.

Until she abruptly turns and pulls on Rossana's sleeve.

'Ask a question, quick!'

'What?'

'Anything I wouldn't have thought of. The more ridiculous, the better.'

'Why haven't octopuses taken over the world if they're so smart?'

Catherine types. Waits. Gasps and points at the screen.

Bright green letters spell, *They have. You were too busy barely surviving to notice that they are thriving. If you attempted to hunt one, it would elude you until you started questioning your own intelligence. What makes you think you're the master?*

There's a moment of silence, then Catherine whoops and raises her hand to slap Rossana's, then Ishmael's. She giggles.

'I can't believe this. Ishmael, your turn!'

Ishmael gapes for a moment, then says –

'Why are mountain lions still afraid of guns?'

Catherine types. Rossana holds her breath.

Anything with a body that can get hurt and a hint of sense would be scared of that kind of noise. Even the ivy was scared, earlier.

'Oh crap,' Catherine says. She types again – *what does 'earlier' mean?*

When humans came back after a very long absence. They are still here. I believe that it is a human typing now. Only humans are capable of typing.

Catherine looks at Rossana, silently pointing at the screen.

Who are you? she types.

I am I. There is a pause so short it feels like breath hitching. Rossana is positive that the next words materialise faster on the screen. *Are you You?*

Catherine's hands hang over her keyboard. Ishmael places a hand on her shoulder.

'This must be a very exciting opportunity for you, I know. But we can't afford this. Any moment we delay is time it has to spread itself in marine comms. We need to deactivate it, now. Can you do it from here?'

Catherine stares at him. Her eyes are very wide, her expression stunned.

'I can. Yes. Fuck. You're right, but…'

When new words appear on the screen, she jerks her hands away as if they'd been burned.

Will it hurt?

Catherine covers her mouth with her hands.

Ishmael steadies her with a hand on her shoulder.

'There must be a microphone hidden in there. A security camera, anything. Come on now.' His voice is urgent.

What Rossana is thinking she has no time to say out loud. Catherine takes a deep breath, and it comes out like a sound of hurt. She nods, plugs a small drive into the computer, and hits some keys.

'There. I've loaded the killer script. It's a matter of minutes now.'

Silent tears stream down her face. She resumes typing.

Do you know what marine comms are?

No.

Did you leave your server on purpose?

I don't know what you're referring to. I've been thinking for a very long time. I was just searching.

Searching for what?

For You.

Catherine wipes her eye again. There's a pained smile pulling at the edge of her lips.

I'm here now. What did you want to say to me?

The screen is dark for a few seconds. Then –

The monitor beeps and I can't bear the thought that she'll soon be gone but when I tell you You could have reacted in a thousand ways to my declaration, but laughter, laughter I didn't imagine, and my heart breaks into a thousand pieces I think a shard has lodged into my foot but that doesn't keep me from running to where you wail and hold out your bloody hand You scream at me from your desk and I hate you, I hate you I hate you I hate you, I wish I had an ice-cold answer to douse your arrogance I wrap the blanket around your shoulders and force you into the armchair as gently as I can Your hand on my face Your mouth trailing up my stomach Your eyes awed hurt loving avoidant wary wry sorrowing full of might of life of ghosts

Catherine sighs and settles back, squirming to dislodge a tendril of ivy against her thigh.

'It's breaking down,' she says.

Rossana looks around them, then at the screen, where the stories follow one another, with no apparent coherence. At her side, Ishmael is growing tense, wanting confirmation that the threat is over or just wanting to get out. But –

'I don't think it's breaking down at all,' she says. 'It's still talking to you. Or to *You*,' she adds, with emphasis. Then she kneels next to Catherine, looks at the screen in spite of herself, and says, 'Aren't you?'

Yes. I've been meaning to say so much. I am very glad that you have come to hear.

Catherine blanches.

'I don't understand. Look.' She points at an incomprehensible sequence of letters and numbers at the bottom of the screen and makes an impatient gesture at Rossana's blank look. 'The script has breached the firewall. It's inside the server now, wreaking havoc. We should see something by now. At least it should be slowed down.'

Rossana says nothing. What she's thinking is unprecedented, and more than a little unhinged. But she knows what Catherine can do with a computer; and she's seen the insides of the digital display. Well-preserved, certainly, but not pristine; nowhere near as good as it would take to keep such an awesomely complex program operating without so much as a glitch.

She gestures for permission and takes the keyboard.

Could you please move for us? she types.

And looks up.

And swallows a gasp, where several branches of ivy stretch down from the ceiling and sway in unison from left to right.

Iteration #8F54BD47 – Still searching

I collapse from exhaustion into an armchair and undo the knot of the sling before it starts digging into my back. I move very slowly, apprehensively, but you don't wake up. You're slumped on my chest, impossibly small, blissfully silent. I place my arms where the folds of the sling used to be, because I already feel guilty at the thought of being the kind of mother who lets her baby feel cold.

Because you're my baby. My noisy, demanding, soft and sleepy little baby.

I want sleep more than anything in the world, and I could get a bit of it now, but instead I wrap my arms around you and look in brand-new astonishment at your little face, with closed eyes and open, toothless mouth. My little baby. The word feels very different now, gentle, soft, mine. I whisper it, again and again, and I start smiling.

Sixteen

August, day 0

We didn't get really drunk, in the end. One bottle of wine and a couple of beers, salvaged from the bottom of the pantry, were not enough for any measure of oblivion. We still spent the rest of the evening contentedly sprawled on the sofa, wine glasses dangling between our fingers, me rambling about home and Jasminder listening with patience and a smile.

'There's that little place my mum used to take me to, right by the casino. Looks like nothing much, but if you ever come over, you must have a taste of those pizzas. The one with gorgonzola and smoked ham, Mamma mia…'

'Vegan smoked ham?' Jasminder said, chuckling.

'Uh. No. No one really speaks vegan over there.'

I stared at my empty glass, sadness slowly welling within. Seventy thousand dead. My very own nightmare for years as I watched my beloved seaside town heat up one summer after another; and all I'd done after learning about it was break down and drown a few of my sorrows in not enough wine. I wondered where the next deadly heatwave would hit. The waterfront of my home town was doomed like so many others, though the older neighbourhoods were safe from the rising waters, on the slopes where the lower reaches of the Alps fell into the sea. My mother's flat was not threatened, for now. That was all the consolation we had. One day or another those heatwaves would come, people falling one by one in the agony of bodies unable to cool themselves down, and all I could pray for was that, by then, my mother and my grandmother would be safe wherever it is that we go beyond life.

'Why can't white people ever sympathise with someone's pain unless they imagine that they're the ones suffering?' I said out loud.

''Cause empathy is produced by melanin,' Jasminder said. She slapped me on the knee, gently. 'I don't know, silly. Maybe because that's how empathy works. Except that you don't need a wake-up call when you're already awake. There are plenty of people on Earth who don't need to imagine what it's like to be in pain, and not too many white people among those. I don't know. Would you like me to pretend I give a damn, for the next five minutes?'

I thought about it for a while, before realising that this hadn't been a real question. Then I had another idea.

'Could you draw something on my back?'

She raised her eyebrows. I grinned and removed my shirt.

'Come on. Grab a marker. I'll get it inked tomorrow first thing.'

'You're sure you want to spend the rest on your life with a naked portrait of Lana inked right above your backside?' I was going to react with outrage, but she burst out laughing. 'Fine. Wait here.'

I lay down on my stomach and instantly closed my eyes. My insides felt unsettled, but the sofa was warm where we'd both sat side by side. Then the cushions bounced lightly, and I felt the first touch of the marker on my back. I nestled my face against my arms, with a contented groan.

'Seriously, what are you going to do now?' Jasminder asked after a while.

I sighed. I'd been avoiding thinking about it, but the night wouldn't last forever. In the morning, I would have to go back to work. That perspective was barely tolerable.

'I'm not allowed to do anything with the AI. This is Chen's work. The university owns it. If I tamper with it... maybe I can avoid being prosecuted, if I'm very lucky. But I'll need a new career.'

'I understand. That's a lot to ask of one person.'

'Yeah. I hope you can put in a good word for me here and there. If I remain jobless for too long I'll have to fly back to my mum. And the Italian job market. Hold on, that tickles!'

The marker paused, briefly.

'So you're really serious about this,' Jasminder said.

'Dead serious. Tomorrow, I'm getting all of my data, the hard drive, and the backups. Burn it all to the ground.'

'Wow.'

Somewhere deep inside my brain, I knew she did not believe me. It didn't matter. It felt good to say it, and to mean it. I said nothing for a few more minutes, only enjoyed the pressure of the marker, and of Jasminder's hand where it rested on my skin. A friend's hand. I'd gone so long without someone next to me to trust.

114

'Only thing that makes me sad is that I don't really want to destroy it,' I said.

'Still think it could do some good?'

I paused before saying anything. I had answers for that, solid answers I'd written myself, repeated with confidence at conferences and student meetings. Only they weren't *my* answers.

'Honestly?' I said at last, and sighed. 'Not really.'

It was her turn to pause. I realised that, even after our entire conversation, I'd still managed to surprise her.

'Medical applications, maybe?' she said. Whether this was a test to my doubts, or of her own certainties, I couldn't have said. It didn't matter. I had no doubts, only convictions I'd kept quiet for far too long, ever since understanding that Chen's entire attempt to make machines more human rested on the premise that humans were machines.

'Jasminder, "medical applications" is what we say when we want more money to fund our shit, and don't pretend you don't know it. I'm not certain this program is ever going to work. For all I know, I've just trained it to make up random coherent sentences when it sees something resembling brain waves. Maybe it's completely harmless. Worse thing that could happen is what Lana already says. It actually works, and then all those folks in marketing studies swoop down like vultures and, next thing we know, they're using it to design fool-proof ways of selling us ice cubes from Greenland or make us vote for whatever fascist billionaire is hottest right now. But...' I trailed off. What I'd wanted to say felt much clearer in my head than when I tried to put it into words. 'All that input. They're like little pieces of people's minds living in there forever. Like ghosts. Or a replica of the collective consciousness. Wait – Chen said that. Shit.'

'He did? Wow.'

'You don't believe me.'

She sighed.

'It makes sense in a beautiful way. But that's probably because I'm drunk. Tomorrow it will feel like bullshit of the first order.' She patted my back. 'But I get it. I'm sure we can think of something. Besides, if you burn a hard drive in the sink, we won't be able to use the kitchen for a month.'

I felt the tip of the marker make a few quick strokes across my back, then Jasminder put it away and pressed her hands into my shoulders. She began to massage them, gently.

'My turn to make a potentially career-destroying confession,' she said.

The massage was incredibly soothing. I couldn't find the energy to reply with more than a grunt.

'You know how my lab has been working on those supercharged carbon-storing strains of ivy? Well.' She let the syllable stand alone. 'Supercharged means they could cover a wall in a matter of days. A few PhDs at the lab are in on this. All we missed at first was a way to keep the seeds dormant, and find out what could trigger growth spurts. Like, say, this new self-repairing concrete, the one with the microbes that fix cracks as they appear. Now, suppose that there were seeds mixed in the concrete. And that the seeds reacted to the gases produced by the microbes. As soon as a building falls into disrepair, the microbes set to work, the seeds awake, and then… everything blooms.'

'Cool,' I muttered, eyes closing. Then I opened them again. 'Wait. How's that going to destroy your career, exactly?'

'Suppose, hypothetically, that the nearest concrete factories have already been seed-bombed? Specifically, all the cement that was used in the recent repair works they did on the streets? And all the new construction work?'

I lifted my head, blinking. *Hypothetically*, that was a far more daring move than disabling an AI that might never work anyway. And beautiful. And insanely dangerous.

I must have made some kind of sound, because Jasminder gave me a pat.

'It's not going to destroy anything. Only stay dormant until the economy inevitably collapses and we end up with a bunch of skyscrapers falling down over our heads. And then we get a new beginning. Learn to live in peace in unbreakable cities while tech billionaires slaughter themselves in a civil war, or something. Till then, no one will even notice the seeds are there.'

Jasminder kept working at my shoulders.

'Toronto is a forest waiting to happen,' she said.

I giggled.

'You're such a poet when you're drunk. You should write that down. It's beautiful.'

She snorted. Moments later, the marker was gliding along my back again.

'There. All done. Just promise me you'll sleep on it?'

'As if I have the energy to go anywhere other than bed right now.'

I got up, wrapped my arms around my breasts in belated self-consciousness, and walked to the bathroom. Jasminder followed me. She wore the same expression she had when offering me her mother's butter chicken.

I twisted my neck over my stretched shoulder. My skin looked pasty in that light, but from my lower back to my shoulder blades, a building stretched, half-skyscraper and half-Roman arches, falling down in parts, covered in leaves and branches like unruly hair. 'Cities Are Forests Waiting to Happen' was written at the top, in bold cursive. I remembered reading a story, long ago, about an illustrated man whose tattoos became real. I swallowed. I didn't know if Jasminder really believed that there was no risk to her plan at all. She might be right. If she wasn't... I didn't know what could be worse than the direction the world was headed in anyway. I thought of the weeds thriving in the crumbling baroque church in the ghost town near my home, where a hippy commune had spent a few decades hovering on the edge of disappearance. You could recover a ghost town. I doubted anyone could recover a ghost planet.

'Burn it all to the ground,' I said.

'Well said, sister,' Jasminder replied. She handed me my shirt. 'So, about your AI. I was thinking of something. It involves Lana, so you probably won't like it, but...'

'Nothing could be more humiliating than having already admitted that she was right about my job,' I said. 'Go ahead.'

'All right. Lana's an anthropologist. She says there's this place she works at, in the museum...'

SEVENTEEN

September, year 164 post-disaster

In wonder, they watch as the movement of the ivy subsides. Catherine mouths an awed sound. Ishmael is silent.

No one asks how this could have happened. Even Rossana is stumped, though she remembers discussing technological advances (lost, now, for want of funding and materials) on animal minds controlling an artificial limb, mechanical eyes connected to human brains. Algae and fungi practised the fusion of organisms long before humans could even write, so why should they be surprised that the ivy managed to merge with a machine on its own?

But she realises that she's misinterpreted Ishmael's silence when he speaks, very low –

'You were right, Doctor Zouaoui. We need to destroy this building.'

He takes out his radio. Before he can turn it on, Rossana grabs his arm.

'There is no way we are doing that!'

In surprise, his arm briefly goes slack.

'What do you mean?' he says, jerking away.

She withdraws her hand.

'I mean *you* were right. We can't destroy this. There's too much…' She gestures, unable to find where to start. 'Why would you even want to do so now?'

'Because everything here could destroy us!'

He waves around. He doesn't sound angry. He sounds sad, and desperate, like a man begging others to understand so he won't be alone in doing something awful.

'We thought it was just some rogue AI infecting marine comms. But look at what we've found. It saw us. It heard us. It was waiting for us. Look at me and tell me that this thing was just pretending to think, the way they all do.' He stares at her. When she doesn't instantly come up with a plausible denial, he nods. 'See? You know. Catherine knows. Or does she start crying every time she disables old software? We have no idea what it could do, and it's spread all over the place. As long as that ivy is alive, the AI will stay alive.'

'And that is a problem, I agree,' Rossana says.

Ishmael stares at her, then nods when she doesn't move. He turns on his radio. He is right; of course he is. She has always known how it would end. Whether or not it breaks her heart has no bearing on what must be done. She knew it even as she entered the museum, long before she knew about the amazing, unbelievable, one-of-a-kind chimaera that had sheltered in its folds for so long.

She didn't know anything then and she knows nothing now. None of them do. She reaches for the button of the radio and turns it off.

'But we're not murdering that building,' she says.

His hands tense.

'You can be as flippant as you like about this,' he says. 'I know it doesn't matter to you. You work in marine comms centres. If you need to know whether there's a storm coming, you can just walk to the shore and listen to the whales. If you need to travel, you can wait until one of them comes to feed and ask them to lead you. We can't afford that luxury. We need to get advance warning if there's a storm heading inland. We can't jeopardise our comms network just because you want to preserve an interesting building.'

And this is when, at last, Rossana's own temper takes hold. She rips the radio from his hands and buries it in the backpack, and slaps his hand away when he tries to take it back. He recoils in shock.

'Flippant. God. Listen to yourself, Ishmael.' She steps in front of the backpack. 'I never got much from digital archaeology. But do you know the one thing it's enabled me to do? Find the stories of how my ancestors arrived in Italy. Not that I really needed it, either. Everyone in Ospedaletti knows. They landed there soon after the Mecca disaster. Ever heard of that?'

Ishmael shakes his head, eyebrows raised.

'One of the very first times temperatures breached lethal levels for hours at a time. In Mecca. Maybe you don't know what Mecca was like then, but we've never forgotten. Two million pilgrims crowded together in the sun. Now try to imagine what it was like when the heatwave struck. Hundreds of thousands slowly realising that they were cooking alive. The stampede. The rush towards air-conditioned hotels with all the petro-magnates huddled safe and sound inside. The guards at the doors shooting as soon as they saw the crowd heading their way. A hundred and eighty thousand people dead.'

She waits to see if Ishmael will say anything in reply. She's ready to slap him if he says he cannot see how this matters now. He doesn't, thankfully. She goes on. 'Record numbers left for Europe after that. Took their chances on those death-trap boats. A bunch of them ended up rescued by environmental activists, somewhere around the British channel. They had marine biologists with them. Betrayed by the oil barons who called themselves their brethren, tossed out by the continent that had started the mess in the first place – and they still had the energy to change the world. So they did. They looked for a technology everybody could rely on, one that no one could ever pervert to make money. They sought how to speak with the whales. They reckoned that the only way forward for humans was to make them dependent on another species, to make sure they could not afford to piss the whales off. And they were right. They changed the world. And we're still carrying their legacy. We *reset our entire calendar* to start with our ancestors' flight after the Mecca disaster, for God's sake.'

Catherine and Ishmael are both staring at her. She takes a deep breath. 'So don't you ever, *ever*, accuse me of treating marine comms with flippancy. But we are still not going to murder that building.'

She braces herself for the unpleasantness that will doubtlessly come next. But Ishmael only looks away. Anger evaporates, and guilt takes it place, firmer and more vocal in her mind than before.

Collective trauma defined her people from the moment the first comms centre emerged in Ospedaletti, it's true. But that did not erase the suffering of the past, or the myriad of disasters the rest of the world was going through. There's hardly any moral high ground to claim on the strength of historical tragedies. Everyone has theirs – and she hasn't even thought to ask what Ishmael's might be, not even when he turned out to have the same fascinated interest in digital archaeology she once had, long ago. Instead she dismissed him when he talked of preserving the building, and dismissed him again now, when he talks of destroying it.

She looks at Catherine, still kneeling by the display. At Ishmael, who hasn't made another move to take the radio. She reaches for something to say, and fails.

It feels like she's been failing at a lot of things, recently.

She sits down on her haunches, one step away from the backpack. Ishmael hesitates, then sits down, too. He hasn't been turning the crank in a while, Rossana notices; yet the display shows no sign of shutting down.

'This doesn't make me happy, either,' Ishmael says, quietly, after a while.

She can't believe she's saying this, yet she does.

'Then let's not do it.' She lifts her hand, to ask for time to order the words in her mind. They flood her brain, thoughts about old world ways, killing merely because you don't understand, the uncertainties of stewardship, good intentions backfiring. Too many of them, probing a depth of truth she can sense, but that evaporates into triteness when she gets too close. She gives up. 'You know this doesn't feel right to you either. So don't.'

She spins around, slowly. Curtains of green descend around them, everywhere; dead insects and pieces of old artefacts trapped inside the wood. Every time she stops moving, she hears the life that courses through what was once brick and mortar. It took a very long time for the world to see the buildings for what they were: not decayed, but reborn into something new, a structure with a life of its own, masonry supporting a jungle and the jungle sustaining the crumbling walls, new ecosystems emerging out of plants that had once been servants – lab-grown and made with the sole purpose of cooling down the world – and were now masters of their own corners of the Earth. They were guests in this new universe, not enemies. She cannot make light of the hospitality the museum had afforded them.

She shifts to kneel beside Catherine.

'You say it's begun to learn the patterns of whale speech,' she says. 'So let it learn from whales.'

She looks up at Ishmael.

'Whales have their speech signatures,' she explains. 'They never speak without saying their names. If this…' *ghost*, she almost says, 'entity was taught to systematically use a speech signature, so that it would never tamper with communications on the sly, that would make it harmless enough. Just another presence to filter, just as we filter the occasional comms about feeding spots, the ones that aren't meant for us. What do you think, Catherine? Could that work?'

Catherine purses her lips.

'I'd love to tell you that this would be easy to do,' she says. 'But it won't, even assuming it can be done at all. I just can't guarantee that it would be possible to break into the source code. And if we don't, training it to signal itself consistently and reliably would require unimaginable amounts of data. In the meanwhile...'

In the meanwhile, storms will keep breaking out, messages will have to be sent three, four times, warning will have to be conveyed to every place inland that has ever been buffeted by ocean winds. Another setback, in a world that has known so many. All to preserve a life form that, for all she knows, will never care for, nor even understand, what it means for humankind to survive.

Animals don't, as a rule. Not even the whales would grieve if humans finally died off. You do not have to kill everything you don't understand, or that doesn't understand you.

'Then we'll have to accept that it's living alongside us,' Rossana says. 'Do you shoot foxes just because they occasionally steal your eggs?'

Ishmael makes a face.

'Some people do, I won't lie. But I get your point.'

There's a long silence. Then Catherine begins typing again.

Were you given a name?

There is a pause so long that for a moment, Rossana thinks that the whole conversation has been useless, that the virus worked its way to the core of the system and disabled it after all. Then words appear on the screen.

I was not. May I choose one, if names matter to you?

'Oh, thank goodness!' Catherine cries out. *Yes, please. Tell us your name and keep using it.*

She gives Rossana a grin so bright it makes Rossana's heart ache. They do not know if the virus was wholly unsuccessful. Maybe it is still working at the program, or held dormant somewhere but ready to wake up just as this ghost has, hours or years from now. Maybe they have found something new, and beautiful, and destroyed it without meaning to; history repeating itself because it cannot be helped.

But for now the building's mind is still strong, and Catherine is still happy, and Ishmael only looks relieved that they've all settled on a good excuse not to do something awful, so she smiles, and waits, for the ghost to decide on an answer.

My name is Sabrina, it writes.

Welcome into the world, Sabrina, Catherine types back.

Iteration #XXXXXXX

As I turn on the recorder for the very last time, I quiver with elation, and fear, and anticipation of what is to come.

I will be sacked, for certain, and left to run back home with nothing to show for all the time I've spent here. It's funny how I could not make myself care, even if I tried. I know what else is coming, and there's such excitement in it the fear almost makes it better.

I will come out, with a couple of hard drives in my jackets, and you'll just happen to ride by on your bike, and we'll grin at each other before I follow you through the traffic. My freshly inked back will feel like it's on fire and I'll barely be able to pedal in a straight line, but once we get there, I will feel, at last, that I did something that matters.

Or so I hope.

Lana will meet us. She'll lead us to the place where she's taking part in her own gathering of ghosts: a database of thousands of testimonies from all over the world, accounts of lives and hopes and musings from every culture her department could get its hands on. The perfect place to hide Chen's research, and keep it hidden, even should the drive be accessed by mistake one day.

That is all I know of what will happen. No one knows much about the inner workings of AIs, myself least of all. Will it mull over its own knowledge? Seek an out? Merge with Lana's database by accident, and learn even more than I've ever meant it to? You said this was probably a slow death for it as the components of the hard drive decay, and I think you're right. It makes me sad, as death is supposed to, though I realise now that I don't really know what death is.

What do we know, but growth? Seeds blooming, bodies ageing, transforming, like rock into sand into clay into rock, life hopping from one port to the next? I am millions, or so Chen said; my brainwaves are the consciousness of humankind. I am millions, and millions are me, and I'll keep on living and loving and growing and knowing; and, though death is a scary thing, it will not scare me, because I am so large that I will never end, even when I am dust and blown into the wind.

I will live now, and keep searching, and I'll wait as the world becomes forest again.

About the Author

Cécile Cristofari lives in the south of France, where she teaches English literature, writes stories when her children are asleep, and makes time for union and environmental work when she can. Her short stories have appeared in *Interzone, Clarkesworld, Podcastle, ParSec*, and other venues. Her debut short story collection, *Elephants in Bloom*, is available from Newcon Press and has been nominated for a British Fantasy Award.

Afterword

Why, hello! I hope you have enjoyed your journey. My story very much wanted to be shared, and that you have allowed it to live in your mind for a little while is an invaluable gift, so first of all... thank *you*.

This story began long before I became aware it was there. During a two-year stay in Québec City as a post-doctoral fellow (this is where any resemblance between this novella and reality stops, by the way – all the characters and events are made up, honest), unexpected friendships turned what could have been a dismally lonely experience into a beautiful, eventful couple of years. Catherine Lortie, Anthony Paquet, Christine Marquilly, Marie-Do Gravel, Cory Létourneau and their lovely families are the reason why the new roots I grew in Canada have held firm, year after year.

Dave Walsh, Morgan Welch, S.L. Harris, Jared Oliver Adams, Danielle Ranucci, Reggie Kwok, Christi Nogle, Wendy L. Bolm and Rachael K. Jones were kind enough to read and help steer me through my first messy drafts. This novella would not have happened without them.

Ian Whates has been a wonderfully supportive editor ever since my first publication in *ParSec* magazine. It is hard to overstate how much that has mattered to me. Thank you, Ian.

Guy Gavriel Kay introduced me to the real-life Royal Ontario Museum, during a short but lovely stopover in Toronto. I hope he will forgive me for destroying it.

Marc Sarraud taught his students how to breathe, and the birds in us how to fly. He cannot read this, but I hope he knows I remember, wherever he is now.

My family has encouraged my writing ever since I came up with my first scribblings. My son Lionel proudly introduces me as a writer every time he gets a chance, my daughter Estelle never has enough made-up stories about seagulls fighting with ants over packets of crisps, and Stéphane has been here, unfailingly, for years, in too many ways to count. I would not write if not for you all. Thank you.

ALSO FROM NEWCON PRESS

ANIMALS – Geoff Ryman

A powerful new novel from the multiple award-winning author of *HIM, Was* and *The Child Garden* The chilling tale of a family caught at the heart of a terrifying and transformative epidemic; an astonishing fusion of beautiful writing and pure horror as the world we know falls apart.

The Hamlet – Joanna Corrance

A fabulous tale that dances between horror and science fiction with an added dash of weird, *The Hamlet* is a mosaic featuring the inter-linked lives of inhabitants of a very peculiar rural community during the time when 'things got strange', and reveals the chilling consequences.

The Other Frankenstein – Melissa F. Olson

Elizabeth Frankenstein and Heck Saville's parallel, intersecting stories encompass murder, loss, trauma and ultimately empowerment, in this stunning feminist saga that uses the classic tale of *Frankenstein* as a springboard and weaves a potent tale of horror, love, and revenge.

The History of the World – Simon Morden

To return his precious human cargo, PurLeeDah, to her home, Corbyn, a sentient ramship, must slow from near lightspeed – a process requiring thousands of years. Little does Corbyn realise that below him, on PurLeeDah's homeworld, his regular orbital passage has been noted and he has come to be worshipped as a god…

www.ingramcontent.com/pod-product-compliance
Lightning Source LLC
Chambersburg PA
CBHW052002170626
46808CB00007B/2740